THE IMPERSONAL LIFE

THE IMPERSONAL LIFE

(Anonymous)

Joseph S. Benner

KALPAZ

ISBN: 978-93-5128-522-9

First Published in 1914
Indian Reprint in 2017

Published by

Kalpaz Publications
C-30, Satyawati Nagar,
Delhi – 110052
E-mail: kalpaz@hotmail.com
Website: kalpazpublications.com
Ph.: +91-9212142040

Cataloging in Publication Data—DK
Courtesy: D.K. Agencies (P) Ltd. <docinfo@dkagencies.com>

Benner, Joseph S. (Joseph Sieber), 1872-1941, author.
The impersonal life / (Anonymous) Joseph S. Benner.
pages cm
"First published 1914"—Title page verso.
ISBN 9789351285229

1. New Thought. 2. Conduct of life. 3. Self-actualization (Psychology) 4. Mysticism. I. Title.

BF639.B46 2017 DDC 299.93 23

INTRODUCTION

In order the better to comprehend the deep and vital truths contained in the within Message, you are urged to approach each reading of it with quiet and open mind. Still the intellect and invite your Soul to do the teaching. Read but a sentence at a time, and do not pass to the next until Something within you responds to the truth therein, and points out clearly the meaning for you.

More than all, try to realize that the "I" speaking thruout the Message is the Spirit within, your own Soul, the Impersonal Self, the *Real* You; the same Self that in other moments of quiet points out to you your mistakes, your follies, your weaknesses, and is ever chiding and aiding you to live up to Its ideals, which It continually holds before your mental gaze.

It was to such a quiet mind as this that the within Message came during months filled with an intense yearning for the guidance of the Spirit and an opportunity to serve the Loving Father who had been found to be ever-present and always ready to bless those of His children who loved Him enuf to make Him first in their hearts and lives.

The help and guidance thus received is passed on to you, for the wise and loving teaching is so unusual and so wholly Impersonal that it will apply equally well to every one who is ready to receive it.

The great blessing of the Message is that, *if you are ready*, the "I" speaking herein will continue to speak direct to *you* from out your own heart, after you lay aside the book, and in so intimate and convincing a way that It will make clear all your problems, be to you a fount of Wisdom and Strength, and bring you Peace, Health, Happiness, Freedom,—everything your *heart* desires.

This little book, therefore, is intended to serve as a channel or open door thru which you may enter into the Joy of *your* Lord, the Comforter promised by Jesus, the living expression *in you* of the Christ of God.

CONTENTS

THE IMPERSONAL LIFE

I.

I AM.

To you who read, I speak.

To you, who, thru long years and much running to and fro, have been eagerly seeking, in books and teachings, in philosophy and religion, for you know not what,—Truth, Happiness, Freedom, God.

To you whose Soul is weary and discouraged and almost destitute of hope.

To you, who many times have obtained a glimpse of that "Truth," only to find, when you followed and tried to reach it, that it disappeared in the beyond, and was but the mirage of the desert.

To you, who thought you had found it in some great teacher, who was perhaps the acknowledged head of some Society, Fraternity or Religion, and who appeared to you to be a "Master," so marvelous was the wisdom he taught and the works he performed;—only to awaken later to the realization that that "Master" was but a human personality, with faults and weaknesses, and *secret* sins, the same as you, even tho that personality may have been a channel thru which were voiced many beautiful teachings, which seemed to you the highest "Truth."

And here you are, Soul aweary and anhungered, and not knowing where to turn.

To *you*, I AM come.

And likewise to you, who have begun to *feel* the *presence* of that "Truth" within your Soul, and seek the confirmation of that which of late has been vaguely struggling for living expression *within*.

Yes, to all you who hunger for the *true* "Bread of Life," I AM come.

Are you ready to partake?

If so, then arouse yourself. Sit up. Still your human mind and follow closely My Word herein spoken. Or you will turn away disappointed once more, with the aching hunger still in your heart.

I!

Who am I?—

I, Who speak with such seeming knowledge and authority?

Listen!

I AM *You*, that part of you who IS and KNOWS;

WHO KNOWS ALL THINGS,

And always knew, and always was.

Yes, I AM *You, Your SELF;* that part of you who says I AM and *is* I AM;

That transcendent, innermost part of you which quickens within as you read, which responds to this My Word, which perceives Its Truth, which recognizes all Truth and discards all error wherever found. *Not* that part which has been feeding on error all these years.

For I AM your *real* Teacher, the only real one you will ever know, and the *only* MASTER;

I, your *Divine* SELF.

I, the I AM of you, bring to you this My Message, My living Word, as I have brought to you everything in life, be it book or "Master," poverty or riches, bitter experience or love, to teach you that I, and I alone, your own True Self, AM The Teacher for you, the *only* Teacher and the *only* God, Who is and always has been providing you not only with the Bread and Wine of Life, but with *all things needed* for your physical, mental and spiritual growth and sustenance.

Therefore *that which appeals to YOU*, as you read, is *MY* Message, spoken to your outer human consciousness from *within*, and is but a confirmation of that which the I AM of you always knew *within*, but had not yet translated in definite, tangible terms to your outer consciousness.

Likewise, *all* that ever appealed to You, coming from some *outward* expression, was but the *confirmation* of My Word already spoken *within*, and which outward expression was the avenue or means I chose at the time thru which to reach and impress your human or self consciousness.

But I AM *not* your human mind, nor its child, the intellect. They are but the expression of *your* Being, as you are the expression of *My* Being; they are but phases of your human personality, as You are a phase of My Divine Impersonality.

Weigh and study carefully these words.

Rise up and free yourself from the domination of your personality, with its self-inflated and self-glorifying mind and intellect, now and for always.

For your mind henceforth must be Your *servant*, and the intellect Your *slave*, if My Word is to penetrate to your Soul consciousness.

I AM come now to your Soul consciousness,

which I have quickened expressly in preparation for the reception of My Word.

Now, if you are strong enuf to bear it;

If you can put aside all your private *personal* fancies, beliefs and opinions, which are but the rubbish you have gathered from the dumping grounds of others;

If you are strong enuf to cast them all away;—

Then My Word will be to you a source of endless Joy and Blessing.

But be prepared to have this personality of yours doubt My Word as you read It all along the way.

For its very life is threatened, and it knows it cannot live and thrive and longer dominate your thinking, your feelings, your going and coming, as of old,—if you take My Word into your heart and permit It there to abide.

Yes, I AM come to you now,

To make you conscious of *My* Presence;

For I have likewise prepared your human mind so that *it* can, in a measure, comprehend the meaning of ME.

I have been with you always, but you did not *know* it.

I have purposely led you thru the Wilderness of books and teachings, of religions and philosophies, keeping ever before your Soul's eye the vision of the Promised Land,

Feeding you with the manna of the Desert, that you might remember and value and long for the Bread of the Spirit.

Now I have brought you to the river Jordan, that separates you from your Divine heritage.

Now the time has come for you consciously to *know* Me; the time has come for you to cross over into Canaan, the land of Milk and Honey.

Are you ready?

Do you *want* to go?

Then *follow* this My Word, which is the Ark of My Covenant, and you shall go over dry shod.

II.

BE STILL AND KNOW.

Now, in order that you may learn to know Me, so that you can be *sure* it is I, your own True Self, Who speak these words, you must first learn to *Be Still*, to quiet your human mind and body and all their activities, so that you no longer are conscious of them.

You may not yet be able to do this,

But I will teach you how, if you really want to know Me, and are willing to prove it by trusting Me and obeying Me in all that I now shall call upon you to do.

Listen!

Try to imagine the "I" who speak thruout these pages as being your Higher or Divine Self, addressing and counselling your human mind and intellect, which you will consider for the moment as being a *separate* personality. Your human mind is so constituted that it cannot accept anything which does not conform with what it has previously experienced or learned, and which its intellect does not consider reasonable. Therefore, in addressing it, you are using such terms and expressions as will most clearly explain to your intellect the truths it must understand before the mind can awaken to the consciousness of your meaning.

The fact is, this "I" *is* yourself, your *Real* Self. Your human mind has hertofore been so engrossed with the task of supplying its intellect and body with all manner of selfish indulgences, that it has never had time to get acquainted with the *Real You*, its true Lord and Master. While You have been so interested in and affected by the pleasures and sufferings of your body and intellect, that you have almost come to believe You *are* your intellect and body, and you have consequently nearly forgotten *Me*, your Divine Self.

I AM *not* your intellect and body, and this Message is to teach you that *You and I are One*. The words I herein speak, and the main burden of these instructions, is to awaken your consciousness to this great fact.

But you cannot awaken to this fact until you can get away from the consciousness of this body and intellect, which so long have held you enslaved. You must *feel* Me *within*, before you can *know* I AM there.

Now, in order that you can become wholly oblivious of your mind and its thoughts and your body and its sensations, so that you *can* feel Me *within*, it is necessary that you studiously obey these, My instructions.

Sit quiet in a relaxed position, and, when wholly at ease, let your mind take in the significance of these words:

Be *still!*—and KNOW,—*I AM*,—God."

Without thinking, allow this, *My Divine Command*, to penetrate deep into your Soul. Let whatever impressions that come to your mind enter at will—without effort or interference on your part. Note carefully their import, for it is *I, within*, thru these impressions, instructing you. Then, when somewhat of their vital significance begins to dawn upon your consciousness, *speak* these My Words slowly, *imperatively*, to every cell of your body, to every faculty of your mind, with all the conscious power you possess:—

"Be *still!*—and KNOW,—*I AM*,—God."

Speak them just as they are herein written, trying to realize that the *God* of you commands and demands of your mortal self implicit obedience.

Study them, search out their hidden potency.

Brood over them, carry them with you into your work, whatever it be. Make them the vital, dominating factor in your work, in all your creative thoughts.

Say them a thousand times a day,

Until you have discovered all My innermost meaning;

Until every cell of your body thrills in joyful response to the command, "Be Still," and instantly obeys;

And every vagrant thought hovering around your mind hies itself off into nothingness.

Then, as the Words reverberate thru the caverns of your now empty being;

Then, as the Sun of *Know*-ing begins to rise on the horizon of your consciousness;

Then, will you feel the swell of a wondrous strange Breath filling you to the extreme of all your mortal members, causing your senses almost to burst with the ecstacy of it; then, will there come surge after surge of a mighty, resistless Power rising within you, lifting you almost off the earth; then, will you feel within the Glory, the Holiness, the Majesty of My Presence;

And then, *then* you will *KNOW*, I AM, GOD.

You,—when you have *felt* Me thus in such moments within, when you have tasted of My Power, harkened to My Wisdom, and known the ecstacy of My all-embracing Love,—you no disease can touch, no circumstance can weaken, no enemy can conquer. For now you *KNOW* I AM *within*, and you always hereafter will turn to Me in your need, putting all your trust in Me, and allowing Me to manifest forth *My* Will.

And you, when you turn thus to Me, will always find Me an unfailing and everpresent help in time of need; for I will so fill you with a Realization of My Presence and of My Power, that you need only *Be Still* and allow *Me* to do whatever you want done,—heal your ills or those of others, illumine your mind so you can see with My eyes the Truth you seek, or perform perfectly the tasks which before seemed almost impossible of accomplishment.

But this Knowledge, this Realization, will not come at once. It may not come for years. And it may come tomorrow.

It depends upon no one but *You*.

Not upon your personality, with its human desires and human understanding.

But upon the I AM of you—God, within.

Who is it that causes the bud to open into the blossom?

Who causes the chick to burst its shell?

Who decides the day and the hour?

It is the conscious, *natural* act of the Intelligence within, My Intelligence, directed by My Will, bringing to fruition My Idea and expressing it forth in the blossom and in the chick.

But did the blossom and the chick have anything to do with it?

No, only as they submitted or united their wills with Mine and allowed Me and My Wisdom to determine the hour and the ripeness for action; and then only as they obeyed the impulse of My Will to make the effort, could they step forth into the New Life.

You may, with your personality, try a thousand times a thousand times to burst thru the shell of your human consciousness.

But it will result only, if at all, in a breaking down of the doors I have provided between the world of tangible forms and the realm of intangible dreams; and the door being open you then no longer can keep out intruders from your private domain, without much trouble and suffering.

But even this I sometimes permit, that you may gain thru such suffering the strength you lack and the wisdom needed to know that, not until you yield up all *desire* for knowledge, for goodness, yes, for union with Me, to benefit self, can you unfold your petals showing forth My perfect Beauty, and throw off the shell of your human personality and step forth into the glorious Light of My Heavenly Kingdom.

Therefore I give you these directions now, at the beginning, that you may be learning how to recognize Me.

For I here promise you, if you follow and strive earnestly to comprehend and obey My instructions herein given, you shall very soon know Me, and I will give you to comprehend *all* of My Word wherever written,—in book or teaching, in Nature, or in your fellow man.

If there is much in what herein is written that seems contradictory, seek out My real meaning before discarding it.

Do not leave a single paragraph, or any one thought in it, until all that is suggested becomes clear.

But in all your seeking and all your striving, do so with faith and trust in Me, your True Self within, and without being anxious about results; for the results are all in My keeping, and I will take care of them. Your doubts and your anxiety are but of the personality, and if allowed to persist will lead only to failure and disappointment.

III.

I, LIFE, GOD.

If that which you have read has awakened a response within, and the Soul of you yearns for more,—then you are ready for what follows.

But if you still question or rebel at the seeming assumption of Divine authority for what is herein written, your intellect telling you it is but another attempt to beguile your mind with cunning suggestion and subtle sophistry,—then you will receive no benefit from these words; for their meaning is as yet hidden from your mortal consciousness, and My Word must come to you thru other avenues of expression.

And it is well if your personality with its intellect impels you thus to question and rebel against authority you do not yet *know* to be Mine. But it is really I Who cause your personality thus to rebel; for your personality with its proud sense of individuality is still needed by Me to develop a mind and body strong enuf that they can perfectly express Me. And until you have become prepared to know Me it is the mission I have given your personality thus to question and rebel. But once you recognize My authority, that moment the undermining of the authority of the personality has begun, and the days of its dominion are numbered, and you will more and more turn to Me for help and guidance.

Therefore, be not dismayed and read on, and mayhap the recognition will come. But know that you can read or not, as you choose; but whichever you do it is really I Who choose, and not you.

For you, who seemingly choose not to read further, I have other plans, and in due season you shall learn that whatever you do, or like, or desire, it is I leading you thru all the fallacies and illusions of the personality, that you may finally awaken to their unreality and then turn to Me as the one and only Reality. Then these words will find a response within:—

"Be *still!*—and KNOW,—*I AM*,—GOD."

Yes, I AM that innermost part of you that sits within, and calmly waits and watches, knowing neither time nor space; for I AM the Eternal and fill all space.

I watch and wait for you to be done with your petty human follies and weaknesses, with your vain longings, ambitions and regrets, knowing that will all come in time; and then you will turn to Me, weary, discouraged, empty and humble, and ask Me to take the lead, not realizing that I have been leading you all the time.

Yes, I sit here within, quietly waiting for this; yet while waiting it was really I Who directed all your ways, Who inspired all your thoughts and acts, impersonally utilizing and manipulating each so as eventually to bring you and My other mortal expressions to a final conscious recognition of Me.

Yes, I have been within always, deep within your heart. I have been with you thru all,—thru your joys and heartaches, your successes and mistakes, thru your evil-doing, your shame, your crimes against your brother and against God, as you thought.

Aye, whether you went straight ahead, or strayed aside, or stepped backward, it was I Who caused you so to do.

It was I Who urged you on by the glimpse of Me in the dim distance I permitted.

It was I Who lured you aside by a vision of Me in some bewitching face, or beautiful body, or intoxicating pleasure, or over-powering ambition.

It was I Who appeared before you in the garb of Sin, or Weakness, or Greed, or Sophistry, and drove you back into the cold arms of Conscience, leaving you to struggle in its shadowy grasp; until you awakened to its impotency, rose up in disgust, and in the inspiration of the new vision tore off My mask.

Yes, it is I Who cause you to do all things, and if you can see it, *it is I Who do all things that you do*, and all things that your brother does; for that in you and in him which IS, is I, My Self.

For I AM LIFE.

I AM that which animates your body, which causes your mind to think, your heart to beat; I AM that which attracts to you pain or pleasure, be it of the flesh, the intellect, or the emotions.

I AM the Innermost, the Spirit, the animating Cause of your being, of all life, of all living things, both visible and invisible; and there is nothing dead, for I, the Impersonal *ONE*, AM *all* that there is. I AM Infinite and wholly unconfined; the Universe is My Body, all Intelligence there is emanates from My Mind, all the Love there is flows from My Heart, all the Power there is, is but My Will in action.

The threefold Force, manifesting as all Wisdom, all Love, all Power, or if you will, as Light, Heat, and Energy; that which holds together all forms and is back of and in all expressions and phases of life, be those phases creative, cohesive or destructive, is but the manifestation of My Self in the act or state of Being.

Nothing can *Be* without manifesting and expressing some phase of Me, Who AM not only the Builder of all forms, but the Dweller in each. In the heart of each I dwell, in the heart of the human, in the heart of the animal, in the heart of the flower, in the heart of the stone. In the heart of each I live and move and have My Being, and from out the heart of each I send forth that phase of Me I desire to express, and which manifests in the outer world as a stone, a flower, an animal, a man.

Is there nothing, then, but this great *I*? Am I to be permitted no individuality for myself? I hear you ask.

No, there is nothing, absolutely nothing, that is not a part of Me, controlled and ruled eternally by Me, the *One* Infinite Reality.

As for your so-called individuality, that is nothing but your personality still seeking to maintain a separate existence.

But soon you shall know there is no individuality apart from My Individuality, and all personality shall fade away into My Divine Impersonality.

Yes, and you shall soon reach that state of awakening where you will get a glimpse of My Impersonality, and you will then desire no individuality, no separation for yourself; for you will see that is but one more illusion of the personality.

IV.

CONSCIOUSNESS, INTELLIGENCE, WILL.

Yes, I know the many mixed thoughts that have been crowding into your mind as you read,—the doubts and eager questionings, the vague fear that imperceptibly changed into a growing hope that this glimmering of My meaning, which has begun to penetrate the darkness of your human intellect, may shine brighter so you can see clearly the Truth which you instinctively feel is hidden beneath My Words.

Again I say, this I AM speaking herein is the Real Self of you, and in reading these words it is necessary that you realize it *is* You, your own Self, that is speaking them to your human consciousness, in order fully to comprehend their meaning.

And I also repeat, this is the same I AM that is the Life and Spirit animating all living things in the Universe, from the tiniest atom to the greatest Sun; that this I AM is the Intelligence in you and in your brother and sister; and that it is likewise the Intelligence which causes everything to live and grow and become that which it is their destiny to be.

But you cannot yet understand how this I AM can be, at one and the same time, the I AM of you and the I AM of your brother, and also the Intelligence of the stone, the plant, and the animal.

You will see this, however, if you follow these My Words and obey the instructions herein given; for I will soon bring to your consciousness a Light that will illumine the deepest recesses of your mind and drive away all the clouds of human misconceptions, ideas and opinions that now darken your intellect,—if you read on and strive earnestly to comprehend My meaning.

So listen carefully.

I AM You, the Real Self of you, All that you *really* are. That which you think you are, you are *not*. That is only an illusion, a shadow of the *Real* You, which is I, your Immortal, Divine Self.

I AM that point of consciousness focalized in your human mind which calls itself "I." I AM that "I," but that which you call your consciousness is in reality *My* consciousness, thinned down to suit the capacity of your human mind. But it is still *My* consciousness, and when you can drive from your mind all its human misconceptions, ideas and opinions, and can cleanse and empty it utterly, so that *My* consciousness can have a chance to *express* freely, then you will recognize *Me* and you will know that you are nothing—being only a focal point of *My* consciousness, an avenue or medium thru which I can express outwardly in matter *My* meaning.

But you cannot see this yet, and of course cannot believe it until I fully prepare your mind by convincing your intellect of its truth.

You have been told that each cell of your body has a consciousness and an intelligence of its own; that were it not for this consciousness it could not do the work it so intelligently does.

But each cell is surrounded by millions of other cells, each intelligently doing its own work and each evidently controlled by the united consciousness of all these cells, forming a *group* intelligence, which directs and controls this work; this group intelligence apparently being the intelligence of the *organ* which the cells comprising it form. Likewise, there are other group intelligences in other organs, each containing other millions of cells, and all these organs making up your physical body.

Now, you know *You* are the Intelligence that directs the work of the organs of your body, whether this directing is done consciously or unconsciously; and that each cell of each organ is really a focal point of this directing Intelligence; and that when this Intelligence is withdrawn the cells fall apart, your physical body dies and exists no more as a living organism.

But who is this *You* who directs and controls the activities of your organs, and consequently of each cell composing them?

You cannot say it is your human or personal self who does this, for you personally cannot of yourself control consciously the action of scarcely a single organ of your body.

It must then be this Impersonal I AM of you, who is You, and yet is not you.

Listen!

You, the I AM of you, are to Me what the cell consciousness of your body is to your I AM consciousness.

You are a cell, as it were, of My Body, and your consciousness (as one of My cells) is to Me what the consciousness of one of the cells of your body is to You.

Therefore, it must be that the consciousness of the cell of your body is My consciousness, even as your consciousness is My consciousness; and therefore We must be *One* in consciousness—the cell, You and I.

You cannot now consciously direct or control a single cell of your body; but when you can at will enter into the consciousness of the I AM of you and know its identity with *Me, then you can control not only every cell of your body, but that of any other body you might wish to control.*

What happens when your Intelligence no longer controls the cells of your body? The body disintegrates, the cells separate, and their work for the time being is finished. But do the cells die or lose consciousness? No, they simply sleep or rest for a period, and after a while unite with other cells and form new combinations, and sooner or later appear in other manifestations of life,—perhaps mineral, perhaps vegetable, perhaps animal; showing that they still retain their original consciousness and but await the action of My Will to join together in a new organism to do the work of the new Intelligence thru which I desire to manifest.

Then apparently this cell consciousness is a consciousness common to all bodies,—mineral, vegetable, animal, human,—each cell fitted perhaps by experience for a certain general kind of work?

Yes, this cell consciousness is common to every cell of every body, no matter what its kind, because it is an *Impersonal* consciousness, having no purpose other than doing the work allotted it. It lives only to work, wherever needed. When thru building one form, it takes up the work of building another, under whatever Intelligence I desire it to serve.

Thus it is likewise with you.

You, as one of the cells of My Body, have a consciousness that is My consciousness, an intelligence that is My intelligence, even a will that is My will. You have none of these for yourself or of yourself. They are all Mine and for My use only.

Now, My consciousness and My intelligence and My will are wholly Impersonal, and therefore are common with *you* and with *all* the cells of *My* Body, even as they are common with all the cells of *your* body.

I AM, and, being wholly Impersonal, My consciousness, My intelligence and My will, working in you and in the other cells of My Body, and which constitute the I AM of you and of them, must work Impersonally,—just as they work Impersonally in the cells of your body. Therefore, I, and the I AM of you and of your brother, and the consciousness and intelligence of all cells of all bodies, are *ONE.*

I AM the directing Intelligence of *All*, the animating Spirit, the Life, the Consciousness of all matter, of all Substance.

And if you can see it, *You*, the *Real* you, the *Impersonal* you, are in all and are one with all, are in Me and are one with Me; just as I AM in you and in all, and thereby am expressing My Reality thru you and thru all.

This will, which you call your will, is likewise no more yours personally than is this consciousness and this intelligence of your mind and of the cells of your body yours.

It is but that small portion of *My* Will which I permit the personal you to use. Just as fast as you awaken to a recognition of a certain power or faculty within you and begin consciously to use it, do I allow you that much more of My Infinite power.

All power and its use is but so much recognition and understanding of the use of My Will.

Your will and all your powers are only phases of My Will, which I thin down to suit your capacity to use it.

Were I to entrust you with the full power of My Will, before you knew how consciously to use it, it would annihilate your body utterly.

To test your strength and more often to show you what the misuse of My power does to you, I at times cause you to commit a sin, so-called, or to make a mistake. I even permit you to become inflated with the sense of My Presence within you, when it manifests as a consciousness of My power, My intelligence, My love; and I let you take these and use them for your own private purposes. But not for long; for, not being strong enuf to control them, they soon take the bit in their teeth, run away with you, throw you down in the mire, and disappear from your consciousness for the time being.

But always I AM there to pick you up, after the fall, altho you do not know it at the time; first shaming you, then straightening you out and starting you onward again, by pointing out the reason of your fall; and finally, when you are sufficiently humbled, causing you to see that these powers accruing to you by the conscious use of My will, My intelligence and My love, are allowed you only, for use in *My* service, and not at all for your own personal ends.

Do the cells of your body, the muscles of your arm, think to set themselves up as having a separate will from your will, or a separate intelligence from your intelligence?

No, they know no intelligence but yours, no will but yours.

After a while it will be that you will realize you are only one of the cells of My Body; and that your will is not your will, but Mine; that what consciousness and what intelligence you have are Mine wholly; and that there is no such person as you, you personally being only a physical form containing a human brain, which I created for the purpose of expressing in matter an Idea, a certain phase of which I could express best only in that particular form.

All this may be difficult for you now to accept, and you may protest very strenuously that it cannot be, that every instinct of your nature rebels against such yielding and subordinating yourself to an unseen and unknown power, however Impersonal or Divine.

But fear not, it is only your personality that thus rebels. If you continue to follow and study My Words, all will soon be made clear, and I will surely open up to your inner understanding many wonderful Truths that now are impossible for you to comprehend. And your Soul will rejoice and sing glad praises, and you will bless these words for the message they bring.

V.

THE KEY.

Now you may not even yet know I AM, or believe that I AM really you, or that I AM likewise your brother and your sister, and that you are all parts of Me and One with Me.

You may not realize that the *Souls* of you and your brother and sister, the only real and imperishable parts of the mortal you, are but different phases of Me in expression in what is called Nature.

Likewise you may not realize that you and your brothers and sisters are phases or attributes of My Divine Nature, just as your human personality, with its mortal body, mind and intellect, is a phase of your human nature.

No, you do not realize this yet, but I speak of it now, that you may know the signs when they begin to appear in your consciousness, as they surely will.

But in order to recognize these signs, all that now follows must be carefully considered and studied, and should not be passed by until My meaning, at least in some degree, is grasped.

Once you understand fully the principle I here set down, then all My Message will become clear and comprehensible.

I first give you the Key that will unlock every mystery that now hides from you the secret of My Being.

This Key, when you once know how to use it, will open the door to all Wisdom and all Power in heaven and earth. Yea, it will open the door to the Kingdom of Heaven, and then you have but to enter in to become consciously One with Me.

This Key is

"To THINK is to CREATE," or

"As you THINK in your HEART, so is it with you."

Stop and meditate on this that it may get firmly fixed in your mind.

A Thinker is a Creator.

A Thinker lives in a world of his own *conscious* creation.

When you once know *how* "to think," you can create at will anything you wish,—whether it be a new personality, a new environment, or a new world.

Let us see if you cannot grasp some of the Truths hidden and controlled by this Key.

You have been shown how all consciousness is One, and how it is all *My* consciousness, and yet is also yours and likewise that of the animal, the plant, the stone, and the invisible cell.

You have seen how this consciousness is controlled by My *Will*, which causes the invisible cells to unite and form the various organisms for the expression and use of the different *Centers* of *Intelligence* thru which I desire to express.

But you cannot yet see how *you* can direct and control the consciousness of the cells of your own body, not to speak of those of other bodies, even if you and I and they are all one in consciousness and intelligence.

By paying especial attention to what follows, however, you now may be enabled to see this.

Have you ever taken the pains to study out what *is* consciousness? How it seems to be an impersonal state of awareness, of waiting to serve or to be directed or used by some power latent in and intimately related to itself?

How man seems to be merely the highest type of organism containing this consciousness, which is directed and used by this *power* within itself?

And that this *power* latent in man's consciousness and in all consciousness is nothing but Will, *My* Will? For you know that all power is but the manifestation of My Will.

Now you have been told that in the beginning I created man in "*My Image and Likeness,*" after which I breathed into him the Breath of Life and he became a Living Soul.

By creating man in My Image and Likeness I created an organism capable of expressing *all* of My Consciousness and *all* of My Will, which means likewise all of My *Power*, My *Intelligence*, and My *Love*. I therefore made it *perfect* in the beginning, patterning it after My own Perfection.

When I breathed into man's organism My Breath, it became alive with *Me;* for then it was I breathed into it My Will—not from without, but —*from within*— from the Kingdom of Heaven within, where *always* I AM. And ever afterward I breathed and lived and had My Being *within* man, for I created him in My Image and Likeness only for that purpose.

The proof of this is, man does not and cannot breathe of himself. Something far greater than his conscious, natural self lives in his body and breathes thru his lungs. A mighty power within his body thus uses the lungs, even as it uses the heart to force the blood containing the life it indrew thru the lungs to every cell of the body; as it uses the stomach and other organs to digest and assimilate food to make blood, tissue, hair and bone; as it uses the brain, the tongue, the hands and feet, to think and say and do everything that man does.

This power is My Will to BE and LIVE in man. Therefore, whatever man is, I AM, and whatever man does, or you do, I do, and whatever you say or think, it is I Who say or think it thru your organism.

Now, you were also told that when man was thus possessed of My Breath he was given dominion over all the kingdoms of the earth. Which means he was made lord of the earth, the sea, the air and the *ethers*, and all beings living in all these kingdoms paid him homage and were subject to his will.

This naturally was so, for I, within man's consciousness and within all consciousness, AM always manifesting My Will; and I, the lord and ruler of man's organism, AM likewise the lord and ruler of all organisms in which consciousness dwells. And as all consciousness is My consciousness and it dwells wherever there is life, and as there is no substance in which there is not life, then My consciousness must be in everything,—in earth, water, air and fire, and therefore must fill all space. In fact it *is* space, or that which man calls space.

Then My Will, being the power latent in all consciousness, must reach everywhere; and therefore man's will, which is but a focalization of My Will, must likewise reach everywhere, and hence the consciousness of all organisms, including his own, is subject to man's direction and control.

All it needs is for him *consciously to realize* this, realize that *I*, the *Impersonal Self within* him, *AM constantly* directing, controlling and using the consciousness of *all* organisms every moment of every day of his life.

And I AM doing this by and thru his *thinking*.

I AM doing this with and thru man's organism. Man thinks *he* thinks. But it is *I*, the Real I of him, who think thru his organism. And thru this *thinking and his spoken word* I accomplish all that man does, and make man and his world all that they *are*.

It makes no difference if man and his world are *not* what *he* supposes they are. They are just what I created them to be for *My* purpose.

But if I do all the thinking, man does not and cannot think, I hear you say.

Yes, here seems a mystery, but it will be revealed to you, if you note carefully what follows:

For I AM going to teach you—man—*HOW to think*.

VI.

THINKING AND CREATING.

I have said that man does not think; that it is I, within him, who do his thinking.

I have also said man *thinks* he thinks.

As this is an apparent contradiction, I needs must show you that man, ordinarily, does *not* think, any more than he does anything else he *supposes* he does.

For I, within him, do *all* that he does; but I necessarily do it thru his organism, thru his personality, his body, mind and soul.

I will point out how this can be.

First, try to realize that I made you in My Image and Likeness, and that I have My Being *within you.* Even if you do not know this now and believe that I, God, AM somewhere without, and that we are separated, try for the time being to *imagine* I AM within you.

Next, realize that which you do when you think is not *real* thinking, because it is not *conscious* thinking; for you are *unconscious* of Me, the Inspirer and Director of every idea and thought that enters your mind.

Next, realize because *I AM within you*, and you are My Image and Likeness, and therefore possess all of My Faculties, you have the *power* of thinking; but not being conscious that thinking is creating and that it is one of My Divine Powers you are using, you have indeed all your life been thinking, but it has all been *mis*-thinking, or what you would call *error*-thinking.

And this error-thinking, this not knowing it is My Power you have been thus mis-using, has been separating you in consciousness farther and farther from Me; but all the time fulfilling My Purpose, which later on will be made manifest to you.

The proof of this is, you *think* you are separated from Me, that you are living in a material World, that your body of Flesh engenders and harbors pleasure and pain, and that an evil influence, called the Devil, is manifesting in the world, opposing My Will.

Yes, you think all these things are so.

And they *are*—to you, for all things *are* to man's mortal consciousness what he *thinks* or *believes* they are.

And I have likewise caused them to *appear* to man to be what he *thinks* they are. This also to suit My purpose, and to fulfill the law of creating.

Let us see if this is not true.

If you *believe* a thing is so, is not that thing really so—to you?

Is it not true that a thing seems real to you, like some sin or evil—so-called, some sorrow, trouble or worry, only because your thinking or believing it so makes it such? Others might see that thing entirely different and might think your view of it foolish. Might they not?

If this is true, then your body, your personality, your character, your environment, your world, *are* what they *appear* to be *to you*, because you have thought them into their present status.

Therefore *you can change them by the same process*, if they do not please you; you can make them whatever you will, by *thinking* them so. Can you not?

But how can one do *real* thinking, *conscious* thinking, so as to bring about this change? you ask.

First know that I, *your Real Self*, purposely brought to your attention these things which now are displeasing and which cause you to *think* them as being what they now *seem* to be to you. And

I, and I alone, AM thus preparing your human mind so that, when you turn within to Me in abiding Faith and Trust, I can enable you to see and bring into outer manifestation the *Reality* of these things which, now *seem* so unsatisfactory.

For I bring to you everything that, by their outer seeming, can attract or lure your human mind onward in its earthly search, in order to teach you of the illusoriness of all outer appearance of material things to the human mind, and of the fallibility of all human understanding; so that you will turn finally *within* to Me and My Wisdom, as the One and Only Interpreter and Guide.

And when you have turned thus within to Me, I will open your eyes and cause you to see that the only way you can ever bring about this change in thinking, is by first *changing your attitude* toward all these things you now think are not what they ought to be.

That is, if they are unsatisfactory or obnoxious to you and affect you so as to cause you discomfort of body or disturbance of mind,—why, *stop thinking* that they can so affect or disturb you.

For who is the master?—Your body, your mind, or *You*, the I AM within?

Then why not show You *are* master, by thinking the *true* things the I AM of you within wishes you to think?

It is only by your *thinking* these other things, by allowing these inharmonious thoughts to enter your mind and by so doing *giving them the power* so to affect or disturb you, that they have any such influence over you. When you stop thinking *into* them this power, and *turn within to Me and allow Me to direct your thinking,* they will at once disappear from your consciousness, and dissolve into the nothingness from which you created them *by your thinking.*

When you are willing to do this, then and then only are you ready to receive Truth, and, by proper *conscious* thinking, directed by Me, to create the true and permanent things I within wish you to create.

Then, when you can thus distinguish the true from the false, the real from the seeming, your conscious thinking will be as potent to create all things you desire, as has been your *un*conscious thinking in the past in creating those things you once desired but now find obnoxious.

For it was by your unconscious thinking, or thinking unconscious of the control your desires exercised over your creative power, that your world and your life are now what you sometime in the past desired them to be.

Have you ever studied and analyzed the process of the working of your mind when a new Idea fertile with possibilities appears?

Have you noticed the relation that Desire bears to such an. Idea, and how, *thru thinking*, that Idea is finally brought to actual fruition?

Let us study this relation and process.

There is always first the Idea, not considering at this moment the necessity or occasion for its appearance. And it matters not from whence the Idea comes, from within or without; for it is always *I* who inspire It or cause It to impress your consciousness at the particular moment it does.

Then, just to the extent that you grow quiet and focus your attention upon that Idea, stilling all the activities of your mind and eliminating all other ideas and thoughts from your consciousness, so that Idea can have full sway, do I illumine your mind and cause to unfold before your mental gaze the various phases and possibilities contained within that Idea.

This takes place, however, up to this point, without any volition on your part, other than focusing or concentrating your attention upon the Idea.

But once I have given your human mind a view of Its possibilities, and have enlisted your interest, then does your human personality take up its task; for as I created and inspired the Idea in your mind, so did I cause that Idea to fructify therein and give birth to Desire,—desire to bring into outer manifestation all the possibilities of the Idea, Desire thus becoming the mortal agent of My Will and supplying the motive Power; just as the human personality is the mortal instrument used to confine and focus that Power.

Yes, all ideas and all desires come thus from Me. They are My ideas and My desires which I inspire in your mind and heart in order to bring them thru you into outer manifestation.

You have no ideas of your own and could not possibly have a desire that came from other than Me, for I AM all there Is. Therefore *all* desires are *Good*, and when thus understood unfailingly come into speedy and complete fulfillment.

You may wrongly interpret My desires, My urges from within, and seek to use them for your own selfish purpose. But even while permitting this they still fulfill My Purpose. For it is only by letting you misuse My Gifts and thru the suffering such misuse brings,—for misuse and suffering are My purifying agents,—that I can make you into the clean and selfless channel I require for the perfect expression of My ideas.

We have, then, first the Idea in the mind; then

the Desire to bring the Idea into outer manifestation.

So much for the relation. Now for the process of realization.

In accordance with the definiteness with which the picture of the Idea is held in the mind, and the extent to which the Idea *possesses* the personality, does its creative Power, impelled by Desire, proceed with Its work. This It does by compelling the mortal mind to *think out* or to imagine (image in), or, in other words, to build mental forms into which I can pour, as into a vacuum, the Impersonal, elemental, vital substance of the Idea, Which, when the Word is spoken, either silently or audibly, consciously or unconsciously, at once begins to materialize Itself, by first directing and controlling the consciousness and all the activities of both mind and body, and of all minds and all bodies connected with or related to the Idea,—for remember, all consciousness, and all minds and all bodies are Mine, and are not separated but are One and wholly Impersonal,—and then so attracting, directing, shaping and molding conditions, things and events that, sooner or later, the Idea actually comes forth into definite, tangible manifestation.

And so it is that every thing, every condition, every event that ever transpired, was first an Idea in the mind. It was by desiring, by *thinking*, and by speaking forth the Word, that these ideas came into visible manifestation.

Think this out and prove it for yourself.

This you can do, if you will, by taking any Idea that comes and following it out thru the above process to realization; or by tracing back any feat you have accomplished, any picture you have painted, any machine you have invented, or any particular thing or condition now existing, to the Idea from which it sprang.

This is the plan and process of all true thinking, and therefore of all Creation.

Listen! *You* have now and always have had, thru this power of thinking, dominion over all the kingdoms of the earth; and, if you but know it, You have now, this moment, only to Think and SPEAK THE WORD, realizing your power, and that I, God, your Omniscient, Omnipresent, Omnipotent Self, will bring about the results, and the waiting consciousness of the invisible cells of all matter upon which your will and attention become focused,—which waiting consciousness is My consciousness, remember,—will begin immediately to obey and do exactly according to the image or plans you have prepared by your *thinking*.

For all things are made by the Word, and without the Word was not anything made that was made.

When you can once realize this and can *know* that the I AM consciousness within you is *one* with the consciousness of all animate and inanimate matter, and that Its will is one with your will, which is My Will, and that all your desires are My desires, then will you begin to know and *feel* Me within, and will acknowledge the Power and Glory of My Idea, which is eternally expressing Itself Impersonally thru you.

But it is first wholly necessary that you learn *HOW to think*, how to know *Your* thoughts, those directed by Me, from the thoughts of others; how to trace thoughts back to their source and to banish undesirable ones at will from your consciousness; and finally how to control and *utilize* your desires so that they will always serve *You*, instead of you being a slave to them.

You have within you all possibilities. For I AM there. My Idea must express, and It must express thru you. It will express itself perfectly—if you but let it; if you will only still your human mind, put aside all personal ideas, beliefs and opinions, and let it flow forth. All you need to do is to turn within to Me, and *let Me direct your thinking* and your desires, let me express whatever I will, you personally accepting and *doing* what I desire you to do. Then will your desires come true, your life become one grand harmony, your world a heaven and your self one with My Self.

When you have begun to realize this and have glimpsed somewhat of its inner meaning, then you will be ready to grasp the real import of what follows.

VII.

THE WORD.

We will now take the Key and show you how the plan and process just described is the one by which the world came into existence, how the earth and all that is in it and on it, including yourself and your brothers and sisters, are but the outer manifestations of an Idea, My Idea, which *is now being thought* into life expression.

First know that

I, the Creator, Am the Original THINKER, the *One* and *Only* THINKER.

As previously stated, man does not think. It is I Who think thru his organism.

Man believes he thinks, but before he has awakened to a realization of Me within he only takes the thoughts I attract to or inspire in his mind, and, mistaking their real meaning and purpose, places a *personal* construction upon them and, thru the selfish desires thus aroused, creates for himself all his troubles and brings upon himself all his woes.

But these apparent mistakes, misconstructions and interferences of man are in reality only the obstacles I place in his way to be overcome, that he may, thru the overcoming, finally develop a body and mind strong and clean and capable enough to express perfectly and consciously this Idea of Mine eternally working within his Soul.

Man, then, is only the organism I AM thus preparing thru which to manifest the perfection of My Idea. He provides the personality, with its body, mind and intellect, thru which I can perfectly express this Idea, the physical brain with which I can think and speak It into outer manifestation.

I plant in man's brain an Idea—any idea. That idea would grow, mature and speedily ripen into complete outer fruition or manifestation,—if man only would let it, would give his mind and all its thoughts, his heart and all its desires wholly over to Me, and let Me come forth as the perfect fulfillment of that Idea.

I will now plant in your brain an idea. May it grow, mature and ripen into the glorious harvest of Wisdom which is awaiting you,—if you *let Me* direct Its growth and expression thru you.

In one of My other Revelations, called the Bible, you are told much about "The Word," but very few, even the most learned Bible students, comprehend clearly My meaning.

You are told that

"In the beginning was the Word, and the Word was with God, and the Word was God.

"The same was in the beginning with God.

"All things were made by him,—by the Word, —and without him—the Word—was not anything made that was made."

You shall learn herein *how* My Word was in the beginning, how It was *with* Me, and how It was *I*, My Self; how all things were made by Me and by My *Word*, and that without Me and My Word was nothing made that now exists.

Now, a word to the human understanding is a symbol of an Idea; that is, it stands for, embodies, and represents an Idea.

You are a Word, a symbol of an Idea, if you can see it. So is a diamond, a violet, a horse.

When you can discern the idea back of the symbol, then you know the soul or the reality of the manifestation *appearing* as a man, a diamond, a horse, a violet.

Hence, a word, as used in the above quotation, means an Idea, an Idea latent and unmanifest, however, waiting to be expressed, or thought and spoken forth, in some *form* or other.

The Word that was in the beginning and that was with Me was then not only an Idea, but It was *My Idea of My Self IN EXPRESSION* in a *new* state or condition, which you call earth life.

This Idea was I, My Self, because It was part of Me, being as yet latent and unmanifest within Me; for It was of the substance and essence of My *BE-ing*, which is Itself an Idea, the One Original Idea.

All things were made by Me by the vitalized action of this, My Idea, being thought and spoken into expression; and nothing has been or ever can be expressed in earth life without having My Idea as the primary and fundamental cause and principle of its being.

This, My Idea, therefore, is now in the *process* of unfoldment or of being thought into outer expression—some call it evolution,—just as is the flower when the bud puts forth from the stalk and finally opens into the blossom, obeying the urge to express My Idea hidden within its soul.

Just so will I develop and unfold all My mediums of expression, which shall finally, unitedly and completely picture forth My Idea from out their souls, in all the glory of Its perfection.

At present these mediums are of such nature that they require many languages of many types, from the simplest to the most complex, composed of almost an infinite number of Words to express My Idea.

But when I shall have completely thought *out* My Idea, or shall have perfected My many mediums of expression, then shall My Idea shine forth in every Word, each, in fact, being a perfect part or phase of My Idea, all so chosen and arranged that they will really be as *one* Word, radiating the sublime significance of My Meaning.

Then shall all languages have melted, merged, into one language, and all Words into One Word; for *all* mediums shall have become flesh, and all flesh shall have become One flesh, the *now perfected medium* for the complete expression *in One Word* of My Idea,—My SELF.

Then shall My SELF, now capable of being expressed by these perfected Words, shine thru Its medium of expression,—thru the personalities, their bodies, minds and intellects; and *the Word shall have become flesh*, or shall *BE the flesh.*

Which means that all Words, thru the regenerative power of My Idea within, shall have evolved *thru* the flesh, transmuting and spiritualizing it and making it so transparent and pure that the personality will have nothing more of earth nature left in it *to hinder* Impersonal expression, enabling My SELF, therefore, to shine forth perfectly and become fully manifest; thus amalgamating once more all Words and all flesh into One Word, *THE WORD, which was in the beginning*, and which then will shine thru all created flesh as the SUN OF GLORY,—The CHRIST of GOD!

This is the *plan* and *purpose* of My Creation and of all manifested things.

A glimpse of the *process* of My Creation, or of My Thinking My Idea of My Self into earth expression, will be given in what follows.

VIII.

MY IDEA.

You have been told that the Earth and all things belonging to it are but the outer manifestations of My Idea, which is now in the *process* of being thought into perfect expression.

You have been shown that My Idea is responsible for all created things, and that It is both the Cause and the Reason for all manifestations, yourself and your brothers and sisters included, all of which have been thought into existence by Me, the One Original Thinker and Creator.

We will now trace the course of that Idea *from the beginning*, thru Its various stages of Earth expression, as well as the process of My Thinking that Idea into Its present state of manifestation.

If you will note carefully all that follows, and will allow Me, within, to direct all of your meditations upon its inner meaning, you will be shown not only the method how to create by thinking anything whatsoever *you* choose to create, but how *you* came into Being and into *your* present state of manifestation.

In the beginning, when, after a rest of incalculable eons, at the dawn of a new Cosmic Day, when the World consciousness was just awakening and the stillness of Cosmic night yet prevailed, I, The THINKER, conceived My Idea.

This My Idea of My Self in manifestation in a *new* condition, called Earth expression, I saw completely pictured in the mirror of My Omniscient Mind. In this mirror I saw the *real* Earth shining forth brilliantly in the Cosmos,—a perfect Sphere, where *all* the Infinite phases, attributes and powers of My Divine Nature were finding *perfect* expression thru the medium of Angels of Light, living Messengers of My Will, My Word in the Flesh, even as it is in the Celestial World of the Eternal.

I saw My Self manifesting outwardly as Nature, and My Life as the vivifying and evolving Principle back of all Manifestation. I saw Love, the Divine Creative Power, as the animating and vitalizing Force back of all Life, and My Desire to give perfect expression to that Love as the Potential and Real Cause and Reason of the birth of My Idea.

All this I saw mirrored in My all-seeing and all-knowing Mind, which could see and reflect only the Soul of things or their Reality. Therefore this that I saw pictured in My Mind was the *Real*

Earth, in fact, its *beginning*, its *conception* into Cosmic being.

Now, My Consciousness is the inner essence of all Space and all Life. It is the *real* Substance of My All-comprehending and All-including Mind, whose informing and vitalizing Center is everywhere and Its limit and circumference nowhere. *Within the realm of My Mind alone* I live and move and have My Being. It both contains and fills all things, and Its every vibration and manifestation are but the expression of some phase of My *Be-ing*.

Be-ing is ex-pressing or out-pressing. You cannot imagine be-ing without ex-pression. Therefore, I, All that is, AM expressing, constantly and continuously expressing.

Expressing what?

What else could I express, if I AM All that Is, but My Self?

You cannot yet see or comprehend Me, My Self, but you can comprehend when I inspire you with an Idea.

Therefore, if I AM All there is, that Idea, *which is direct from Me*, must be part of or a phase of My Self in *Being* or Expression.

Any Idea, once born within the realm of *My*

Mind, as has been shown, immediately becomes a Reality, for in the Eternality of My Being Time is not. With you, however, an Idea first creates Desire, a desire to express that Idea; then Desire compels Thinking, Thinking causes Action, and Action produces Results—the Idea in actual outer manifestation.

But in Reality I have no Desire, for *I AM All Things*, and All Things are *of* Me. I need only to *think* and Speak the Word to produce results.

Yet that Desire you feel in you is from Me, because it is born of My Idea, which I emplanted in your mind only that it might come forth into expression thru you. Indeed, whatever you desire is I, knocking at the door of your mind, announcing My purpose of manifesting My Self in you or thru you in the particular form indicated by that Desire.

What is called Desire in human personalities, is but the necessary Action of My Will pushing forth the expression of My Idea into outer Manifestation or Being.

What to you would seem to be in Me a desire for expression, is but the *Necessity* of My Idea of My Self to *Be*, or Express Itself.

Therefore, every *real* desire you feel, every desire *of your heart*, comes from Me and must of necessity sometime, in some shape or other, be fulfilled.

But as I have no Desire, because I AM All Things, once this Idea of expressing My Self in this new condition was born, I had but to *think*, that is, to concentrate or focus My Attention upon My Idea and Will it to come forth into expression, or, as is told in My other Revelation, to Speak the Creatve Word, and at once did the Cosmic Forces of My BE-ing, set in vibration by the concentrating of My Will, proceed to attract the necessary elements from the eternal storehouse of My Mind, and, with My Idea as a nucleus, to combine, form and shape around it these elements into what is called a thought-form of a planet, filling it with My Life Substance—My Consciousness—and endowing it with all the potentialities of My Being.

But this act of thinking produced only a vitalized *thought-form* of a planet, and its manifestation was still in a nebulous state in the thought realm.

From a thought-form, however, the quickening power of the Idea within, with My Will focused upon It, proceeded to mold, fashion and gradually to solidify into material form the various elements of Life Substance; until My Idea finally shone forth in substantial manifestation in the world of visible forms as the planet Earth, a medium ready for living expression, and now capable of both containing and expressing Me.

This was the material body prepared by My Thinking, in which already dwelt all the *potential* nature of My Being, by reason of the informing power of My Idea within.

The next stage was the developing and preparing of avenues or mediums thru which I could express the manifold phases, possibilities and powers of My Idea.

The outward evidence of this was what is known as the mineral, vegetable and animal kingdoms, which, each in turn, as it came into manifestation, gradually unfolded higher and more complex states of consciousness that enabled Me more and more clearly to express the infinite phases and variety of My Nature.

It was at this stage that I looked upon My Creation, as stated in My other Revelation, and saw that it was good.

But there yet remained the final and culminating medium of expression.

Up to this point, while each perfectly expressed some phase of My Nature, yet all existing mediums and avenues were unconscious of Me, and were mediums of expression only as a wire is a medium for conducting heat, light and power.

The conditions were now ripe, however, for the creation of mediums thru which *My Divine Attributes* could find *conscious* expression, conscious not only of their relationship to Me, but of their ability and power to express My Idea.

It was at this moment in Time that You and Your Brothers and Sisters were born into existence as human expressions, coming into manifestation as you did, similarly with all other mediums, in response to My concentrated Thought, in which I saw all the infinite variety of My Attributes in actual expression in entitized forms, each manifesting in predominance some particular phase of My Being, and each conscious of Me, Its Creator and Expressor.

I saw *You* in perfect expression, even as I see *You* now—the *Real* You, an *Attribute* of *My Self* —*perfect.*

For in Reality *You* are an Angel of Light, one of My Thought Rays, an Attribute of My Being, ensouled in Earth conditions, with no other purpose (which is no purpose at all, but a necessity of My Being) but the final complete expression of My Idea.

In the Eternal there is no Time, or Space, or Individuality, and it is only by reason of the phenomenon of Thought being born from the womb of Mind into the world of Matter that the illusions of

Time, Space and Individuality occur, the Thought, or Creature, attaining the consciousness of separateness from its Thinker or Creator.

So it was then that the first tendency to *think* yourself as separate from Me was born. But the complete consciousness of separation did not take place until long after.

In the beginning, when You thus first entered into Earth expression, obeying the impulse I had sent forth thru My concentrated Thought, You, one of My Attributes, surrounded or clothed Your Self with *My Idea* of My Self in expression as the particular Attribute You represented, You being the animating Force of that Idea.

In other words, My Idea of My Self expressing that particular Attribute then became the *Soul* of Your particular expression. But that Idea or Soul is not You, remember, for You are really a part of Me, being My Self in expression thru the medium of that particular Attribute.

Having clothed Your Self with My Idea, this Idea then, thru the necessity of Its be-ing, immediately began to attract to Itself the necessary *Thought Substance* requisite for the *expression* of that particular Attribute, and to build and shape it into My Image and Likeness. It thus became a

Holy Temple, filled with My living Presence, because inhabited by You, one of My Divine Attributes.

This Temple, being in my Image and Likeness, and composed of My Thought Substance, surrounding and clothing My Idea, is consequently your *Real* body. It is therefore, indestructible, immortal, *perfect*. It is My complete, imagined (imaged in) Thought, containing My Living Essence, awaiting the time when it can come into outer expression and take on material form.

So now we have,—

First, *I AM*, expressing as *You*, one of My Divine Attributes;

Second, *My Idea* of You, one of My Attributes, expressing in Earth conditions—or *Your Soul;*

Third, *My Imaged Thought* of You, forming the Temple of Your Soul—or *Your Soul Body*, in which You dwell.

These three make up the Divine or Impersonal part of You, the Immortal *Three-in-One*—You, My latent yet completely formulated thought, shaped in My Image and Likeness, as yet unquickened, and therefore having no connection with your human personality, which has not yet been born.

IX.

THE GARDEN OF EDEN.

Whether or not you have gotten any clear grasp as yet of what has just been stated, do not discard it as impossible of comprehension. For in every line is hidden a meaning that will more than repay you for the study necessary to make it become clear.

This Message is to awaken you to a realization of what *You* are, to a realization of your *real* Self. It is intended to make you once more conscious of Me, your Divine Self, so conscious that never again will you be deceived by that other self, which you have imagined as being you and which so long has lured you on by feeding you with its unsatisfying sense pleasures, its mental dissipations and emotional delights.

But before that can be it will be necessary for you thoroughly to know that supposed other self, that self which You created by *thinking* it real and *separate* from Me, and then kept alive by giving it the power thus to entice and deceive you; yes, that self-created self, with its purely selfish pride and ambitions and imagined power, its love of life, of possessions, of being thought wise or good,—but which self is merely your human personality, which was born only to die as a separate identity, and as such has no more reality or permanence than the leaf, the snow or the cloud.

Yes, you will be brought face to face with that petty personal self, and will see with perfect vision all its sordid selfishness and human vanities; and you will then learn—if you will but turn to me and ask in simple faith and trust—that it is *I*, the Infinite, *Impersonal* part of You, abiding always *within*, who am thus pointing out to you all these illusions of the personality, which for so many ages have separated you in consciousness from Me, Your glorious, Divine Self.

This realization will surely come, when you can recognize that this Message is from Me, and when you have determined that it shall be. To you, whom I have inspired with such a determination, I will cause *every* illusion in time to disappear, and you shall in truth *know* Me.

The exercise of your mind along these abstract lines will not hurt you. Instead it is what your mind needs. For, not until you can grasp My Meaning when presented to you in ideas such as these herein contained, coming from without, can you perceive and correctly interpret My Idea when

I inspire you from within. Your mind I AM thus preparing for USE, not to gain more earthly knowledge, but in order that you can receive and *give forth* My Heavenly Knowledge to those whom I shall bring to you for that purpose.

So with a prayer to Me, Your own Real Self, your GOD within, that true realization may come, and that you may see the Truth in these statements, and in all things, conditions and experiences that may come to you, let us proceed.

We have arrived, in the course of our consideration of the process of unfoldment of My Idea, to where the I AM of you, manifesting in your Immortal Soul Body, or in the Thought Image created by My Thinking, is now ready to enter into material form, a form suitable for the earth expression of My Attributes.

This change from a mental to a mortal form took place after the manner and process of all thinking and all creating, and is literally described in the Bible, where it says I "formed man of the dust of the ground, and breathed into his nostrils the breath of life; and man became a living soul."

Shall I explain further?—That the quickening power within My Idea (your Soul) proceeded to attract to it the various elements of life substance (dust), and, atom by atom, and cell by cell, in due course of time, to mold and shape each into bone, tissue and organs, after the pattern of the Thought Image composing your Soul Body, thus forming an earthly outer covering, as it were,—until finally your mortal form actually became *manifest* to the psychic sense of the outer world, if not yet to the physical eye. Whereupon, all being now prepared for this cyclic moment, You, My Attribute, breathed into and then thru its nostrils (from within) the breath of life, and *You* then made your first appearance on earth as a tangible *human* being—a *living* Soul (My Idea now able to express consciously thru a suitable earth medium), containing within your Self all of My Attributes, all of My Powers and all of My Possibilities.

Thus were now manifest all the various mediums for the Earth expression of My Idea; and You, being one of My Attributes, naturally had dominion over all of these mediums, or possessed the power of utilizing any or all of them, if necessary, for the full and complete expression of *Your*—My Attribute's—powers and possibilities.

In this manner and for this reason alone did You and Your Brothers and Sisters come into human expression. But while in human form yet was Your expression so entirely Impersonal, that, tho self-conscious, you still looked wholly to Me within for inspiration and guidance.

This, then, was the first condition into which You awakened when You entered into Earth expression, and is what is called the Edenic state or dwelling in the Garden of Eden.

This Edenic state represents the Celestial phase of Impersonal Consciousness, or that state in which You were still consciously One with Me, tho now confined in a mortal medium of expression.

Now, I shall not tell you in detail how or why it became necessary for Me to "drive" You (now manifesting as Man or Humanity) out of the Garden of Eden, other than to remind you of the part that Desire plays in Earth expression, and its relation to My Will; how it centers your interest in outer things and makes you forget Me within.

When you have solved that and comprehend somewhat of My reason, then perhaps you can understand the necessity of first causing Your (Humanity's) consciousness to fall into a deep sleep (You having approached the close of another Cycle, called a Cosmic day), and of letting you think you had awakened—but in reality you were still asleep and only dreaming,—and of finding Your Self (Humanity) no longer outwardly one, but two; one an active, thinking, aggressive part, thereafter called a man, and the other a passive, feeling, receptive part,—a womb-man, or woman;

Also the necessity of some Earth or outer influence being brought to bear to draw Your consciousness from purely Celestial delights and to hold it in this new dream condition, in order to develop a mortal mind, that You might thru its natural selfish tendencies become centered entirely upon Your earthly mission of mortal expression;

And the wisdom of having this influence, thru the Serpent of Selfishness (the shape I caused it to assume in your mind), first generate in the passive, feeling, receptive part of You—*Desire*, the mortal agent of My Will, which was to supply the motives and the power for the further and complete expression of My Attributes on Earth;

And finally the necessity of Desire casting its complete spell over You (Humanity), that Your Celestial or Impersonal nature might be kept entirely in abeyance; until, by the free but ignorant use of My Will, You could taste and fully eat of the *fruit* of the so-called Tree of Knowledge of Good and Evil, and thru the eating could learn properly to discriminate and know its fruit for what it really is; and thus acquire the strength to use the knowledge thus gained wisely and perfectly in the expression of My Idea only.

You likewise possibly now can understand how Your (Humanity's) eyes became opened to earthly or outer things, thru the first eating of this fruit and learning to know Good *and* Evil, and, after learning of the new and enticing world thus opened up to you, dying to the knowledge of the Reality back of it all; and how and why it was You learned that You were naked—both the thinking and the feeling parts of You; and also why you grew afraid.

And now, perhaps, you can see why this all had to be, why You (Humanity) had to leave the Edenic state of Impersonal consciousness and lose Your Self wholly in these outer conditions portrayed so alluringly by Desire in this Dream World, in order to be able to create a body and develop in it a personal or self consciousness capable of fully expressing My Perfection.

Thus was born Your human personality, and since its birth have I impelled You to nourish, support and strengthen it, by filling You with longings, hopes, ambitions, and aspirations, with *all* the various manifestations of Desire; and which are but the human phases of My Will, operating in the preparation and development of a medium capable of expressing perfectly My Attributes on Earth.

And so I Spake the Word, and drove You out of the Garden of Eden, and clothed You with a "coat of skin," or, in other words, with flesh, the same as other animals. For now, in order that You might enter into the heart of Earth conditions, into the *real* Earth, the Earth of My Idea,—not the one of your Dream,—so as to quicken My Idea therein into active *life* expression, You, My Attribute, had to have an organism and a covering appropriate for the conditions in which You were to manifest.

Likewise, in thus giving You a coat of skin, or a physical organism, did I, by so doing, provide My Idea with a suitable form for earthly expression,—I gave you the power to express Your Self, thru a physical organism, by means of words.

In the Impersonal there is no use or necessity for words. Ideas alone exist and express. They simply *Are*, for they are the expression of the various phases of My *Being*.

But in this new condition, where every expression in these early stages of outer being had to have a form and substance that could be heard, seen, felt, smelled or tasted, in order that its meaning could be clearly apprehended, there naturally had to be provided organisms capable of being used for the double purpose of expression and of understanding what was expressed.

As My Idea unfolded Itself, after Your expulsion from Eden, You—one of My Divine Attributes, dwelling within My Idea of that Attribute in expression, in turn dwelling within the Thought Image of My Self, and finally manifesting outwardly in the Earth form of Words, when impelled by My Will in the guise of Desire to express My Meaning—began rapidly to "increase and multiply."

And in Your search for the most favorable conditions for the manifestation of Your particular attributes, You gradually spread over the face of the Earth, quickening and arousing the Intelligence dormant in all forms of life contacted into fuller and more active expression of their particular phases of My Idea.

Thus were formed the various Languages of Earth, each containing many words, and all born of Desire in the human mind to express in Earthly terms the infinite phases of My Idea ever surging within.

And the more the *human* mind strove thus to express—in Words—My Idea, the greater and more abject the failure.

And in time will the Great Awakening come—that all Words are but Symbols of One Idea—and all Ideas of whatsoever nature are but phases of One Idea, My Idea of My Self in Expression, and that all Desire to express in Words that Idea, without the consciousness of My Will being the One and Only source of Inspiration, is futile. And likewise, all desire to express in *living acts* that Idea, without losing all consciousness of your human personality—of your personal part in the acts, and centering your self wholly in Me, is vain and fruitless, and will end only in failure, disappointment and humiliation.

X.

GOOD AND EVIL.

In the Garden of Eden, where you abode before entering upon your earthly mission, there grew this tree whose fruit is called the Knowledge of Good and Evil.

While dwelling in this Garden you were still wholly Impersonal, for you had not yet tasted of this fruit. But having once yielded to Desire, the earthly agent of My Will, whose main work is to make you eat this fruit, the moment you had eaten, that moment you descended, or fell, or were forced from your Edenic estate (like the chick from the shell or the rose from the bud), and you found yourself involved in conditions altogether new and strange. For now, instead of having dominion over the lower kingdoms, and of their supplying your every want, you had to till the ground to get it to bring forth fruit, and by the sweat of your brow had you to earn your bread.

But having taken upon yourself this earthly mission, it now became necessary for you to enter fully into all conditions of earth life, in order to develop a mind and perfect a body capable of expressing perfectly My Idea on Earth,—the real cause and reason of your entering into this new condition.

So having fallen or stepped out of your Impersonal or Edenic estate, you yielded completely to the lure of this Dream World, and now permitting Desire wholly to lead, you no longer were capable of seeing the Reality or Soul of things; for you had put on a physical body, an earthly covering with a human brain, which, because influenced by Desire, acted as a veil to your Soul Consciousness, and so bedimmed your sight and clouded your mind that the light of Truth could not penetrate thru, and everything was falsely colored and distorted to your human understanding.

And you saw all things darkly, as thru a mist, and this mist enshrouding everything you could not see things in their Reality, but only their misty *appearance*, which now however seemed to you the *real* things themselves.

This was so with everything you saw thru your physical eyes, with things both animate and inanimate, with everything you conceived in your human mind, with even your own Self and your other Selves round about you.

Thus no longer seeing the Soul of things, but only their misty shadows, you grew to thinking these shadows were real substance, and that the world about you was composed of and filled with such substance.

But this mist was only the effect of the Light of Truth being unable to penetrate thru your human mind, whose intellect, like an imperfect lens, only befogged and twisted everything and made it *appear* as Real, keeping your consciousness continually busied with these myriad illusions of your Dream World.

Now the intellect is a creature of and wholly controlled by Desire, and is not, as many suppose, a faculty of the Soul. In other words, this mist then was the clouded lens of your human intellect, which, because controlled by Desire, falsely portrayed and interpreted to your consciousness every image, idea and impulse I inspired from within or attracted from without, during the process of My awakening your consciousness to a recognition of My Idea within ever urging for outer expression.

All this I did purposely, however, thru the agency of Desire, in order to lead you consciously into the heart of earth conditions.

And while this false vision, inspired by Desire, caused many mis-steps and much trouble and suffering, and you gradually lost confidence in your Self—in Me, the Impersonal One within,—in fact, you forgot Me,—so that you did not know where to turn in your helplessness; yet it was only thru your thus losing the memory of your Divine estate, and centering *all* your consciousness in these earthly conditions, that I could develop your human mind and will, and all your faculties, and provide your human body with the strength and powers that would enable Me to give perfect expression to My Divine Idea on Earth, which eventually must BE.

And so, thru your mistakes and troubles and sufferings, Desire for relief caused the Idea of Evil to spring up in your mind, and likewise when these troubles were not It inspired the Idea of Good.

And to all *appearances* of things and conditions you attributed these qualities of Good or Evil,—according to whether or not they satisfied Desire, My Agent, in Realty My *human Self*, or *You*, in your human personality.

But all these conditions and experiences in life which you entered into, and when pleasing seemed Good, and when displeasing seemed Evil, were merely incidents created by Desire to quicken in you certain Soul faculties, which would enable you to recognize the Truths that I, within, wished at the time to impress upon your consciousness: the apparent Evil being the *positive* aspect of the Fruit of the Tree, which always lured you on by its fair appearance and by the sweetness of the first taste to eat and enjoy to satiation, or until its harmful effects manifested and became a curse, bringing final disillusionment; which served to turn or force you back in shame and humiliation to Me, your True Self, Who, thru the new consciousness thus aroused, was then enabled to extract the Essence of the Fruit and incorporate it into Soul substance and tissue.

And the apparent Good being the *negative* aspect of the Fruit, which, having pushed forth of itself into expression, thru your recognition of and obedience to its urge, was now permitting you to enjoy its happy and natural *effects*, and to receive the outward benefits of *My* loving inspiration and guidance.

But this *you*, who were being led by Desire thru all these experiences, was only your human personality, which the *Real* you was training and developing and preparing so it could become a perfect instrument for Your *use* in the expression of My Idea, ever seeking to manifest forth Its perfection in the flesh.

And all this *You* did, not only compelling your human personality to eat but to *live* on the *fruit* of the so-called Tree of Knowledge of Good and Evil, until you had seen and known *all* the so-called Evil, and from living *on* and *with* it had discovered *in* it the germ of so-called Good, plucked it, lifted it up, and turned it right-side out; so that you from that time on knew that Good and Evil had no real existence, and were but relative terms descriptive of *outside* conditions looked at from different viewpoints, or were only different outer aspects of a central *inner* Truth, the *Reality* of which was what *You* sought to Know, Be and Express.

And so during the latter ages you have been, as it were, gradually throwing off layer after layer of human consciousness, dissipating the mist or glamour thrown around your mind by the intellect; subduing, controlling, spiritualizing, and thus clarifying the intellect itself; until now you are beginning to awaken and to see, thru the ever thinning remaining layers, occasional glimpses of Me, the one Great Reality, within all things.

But all this time, *You*, the Omniscient, Impersonal I AM of You, were consciously and intentionally doing all this; not for the purpose of getting the mere knowledge of earth conditions and things, as your Intellect has so loudly and authoritatively proclaimed, but in order that you might harvest what You had sown in the dim ages past, and could manifest forth My Perfect Idea on Earth, even as You are now manifesting it in the Impersonal estate, Your Heavenly Home.

And You, remember, are the Great Impersonal I, Who AM doing all this, Who AM continually changing in outward appearance, but Who within AM eternally the same.

The endless flow of the Seasons,—the Spring, with its busy sowing; the Summer, with its warm, restful ripening; the Autumn, with its bounteous harvesting; the Winter, with its cool, peaceful plenty, year after year, life after life, century after century, age after age—are only the outbreathing and inbreathing of My Idea as I inspire It forth thru the Earth and thru You, My Attribute, and thru all My other Attributes, during the process of unfolding in outer manifest state the perfection of My Nature.

Yes, I am doing it thru You, because You are part of Me, because only thru You, My Attribute, can I express My Self, can I BE. I AM because You Are. You ARE because I AM expressing My SELF.

I AM in You as the oak is in the acorn. You are I as the sunbeam is the Sun. You are a phase of Me in expression. You, one of My Divine Attributes, are eternally trying to express My perfection thru Your mortal personality.

Just as an artist sees in his mind the perfect picture he wants to paint, but his hand cannot quite portray with the crude mediums of brush and color the true quality and effect he sees, so do You see Me within Your Self and know We are One, but always are prevented, by the imperfection of the earthly material of your human personality, with its animal body, its mortal mind, and selfish intellect, from perfectly expressing Me.

Yet, I created your body, mind and intellect, in order to express My Self thru you. The body I made in the image of My Perfection; the mind I gave to inform you of Me and My works; the intellect I gave to interpret My Idea as I inspired it to the mind. But you have been so distracted by the *human* phases of this body, mind and intellect, and their outer uses, that you have forgotten Me, the One and Only Reality within, Whose Divine nature I AM ever seeking to express to and thru you.

But the time is soon here when the outward uses shall no longer distract, and My Reality shall be revealed unto you in all the glory of Its perfection *within* You.

But You, when I thus reveal My Self, shall not be more blessed than before, unless that which I have revealed shall become the Bread of Life to you, and you shall live and *manifest* the Life It reveals.

XI.

USE.

Now I have purposely not stated clearly all the how and why of these things; for I have reserved for you, when you call upon Me so to do, and are capable of receiving it, to inspire you *from within* with a far more comprehensive vision of the unfoldment and development of My Divine Idea, and Its final perfected expression, than is herein pictured.

If I were here to tell the *real* meaning of My many manifestations, before you were consciously capable of experiencing its Truth, you neither would believe My words, nor could you comprehend their inner application and use.

Therefore, as I begin to awaken in you a realization that I AM within, and more and more cause your human consciousness to become an Impersonal channel thru which I can express, will I gradually reveal to you the Reality of My Idea, dissipating one by one the illusions of the ages which have hidden Me from you, enabling Me thereby to manifest thru you My Heavenly Attributes on earth in all their humanly Divine perfection.

I have herein given you but a glimpse of My Reality, but just to the extent that that which has been revealed becomes clear will more be opened up unto you from *within*, and far more wonderful than these now seem to you.

For My Idea within, when It finally and completely shines thru its mantle of flesh, will compel you to worship and glorify Me far above all that your human mind and intellect now conceives as God.

But before you can become conscious of all this and can truly comprehend it, you and your human personality must make it possible for Me to reveal it, by turning within to Me as the *One* and *Only* Source, bringing to Me your measure absolutely empty of self, and with mind and heart as simple and trusting as those of a child.

Then and then only, when nothing of the personal consciousness remains to prevent My filling you full to overflowing with the consciousness of Me, can I point out to you the glories of My Real Meaning, for which this whole Message is but the outer preparation.

The time has now arrived, however, for you to comprehend somewhat of this. Enuf has been revealed to prepare you for the recognition of My Voice speaking within.

Therefore, I shall now proceed as if you realize I AM within, and that these Truths which I voice thru the medium of these pages are but to impress more strongly upon your consciousness those phases of My Idea which you could not clearly receive direct.

That which herein appeals to you as Truth is consequently but a confirmation of that which My Idea has heretofore been struggling to express from within.

That which does not appeal and which you do not recognize as your own, pass it by, for that means I do not desire you to receive it as yet.

But each Truth I voice herein will go on vibrating until it reaches the minds I have quickened to receive It; for every word is filled with the potent power of My Idea, and minds that perceive the Truth hidden therein, to those minds this Truth becomes a living Reality, being that phase of My Idea they are now worthy and capable of *expressing.*

As all minds are but phases of My Infinite Mind, or parts of It manifesting in different forms of mortal nature, when I speak thru the medium of these pages to your mind and to other minds, I AM but speaking to My mortal Self, thinking with My Infinite Mind, pushing forth My Idea into earthly expression.

Just so will *You* soon be thinking *My* Thoughts, and be conscious that I AM speaking within direct to your human consciousness, and you will then no longer have to come to this book or to any other of My *outer* Revelations, either spoken or written, in order to perceive My Meaning.

For AM I not within You, and AM I not You, and are You not One with Me, Who live in and express thru the consciousness of all minds, knowing all things?

And all that remains for you to do is to enter into the All-consciousness of My Mind and abide there with Me, even as I abide within My Idea in Your Mind; when all things shall be Yours, as they now are Mine, being but the outer *expression* of My Idea, and existing only by reason of the consciousness I gave them when I thought them into being.

It is all but a matter of consciousness—of your conscious thinking. You are separated from Me only because you *think* you are. Your mind is but a focal point of My Mind. If you but knew it, what you call *your* consciousness even is My consciousness. You cannot even think, much less breathe or exist without *My* consciousness being in you.—Can you not see it?

Well, then, *think*, *believe* you are I, that We are not separated, that we could not possibly be separated; for we are ONE,—I within You, and You within Me. Think this is so; determinedly *image* it as so; and verily the moment you *are conscious* of this, that moment are you with Me in Heaven.

You are what you *believe* you are. Not one thing in your life is Real or has any value to you only as your *thinking* and *believing* has made it such.

Therefore, *think* no more you are separated from Me, and abide *with* Me in the Impersonal Realm, where all Power, all Wisdom, and all Love, the threefold nature of My Idea, but await expression thru You.

Now I have spoken much of this, and have apparently said the same thing more than once, but in different words. But I have done this purposely, presenting My Meaning in different lights, that you might finally be brought to comprehend My Divine Impersonality, which is in Reality *Your* Impersonality.

Yes, I have repeated and will continue to repeat many Truths, and you may think it tedious and unnecessary; but if you will read carefully you will find that each time I repeat a Truth I always add something to what has already been said, and that each time a stronger and more lasting impression is made upon your mind.

If that is so, My purpose has been accomplished, and you will soon come into a *Soul* realization of that Truth.

But if you receive not such impression and still think such repetition a useless waste of words and time, know that your intellect only is reading, and that My *real* meaning has altogether escaped you.

You, however, who do comprehend, will love every word, and will read and re-read many times, and consequently will get all the wondrous Pearls of Wisdom I have in reserve for you.

And this book and its message will be to you hereafter merely a fount of inspiration, or a door thru which you will be enabled to enter into the Impersonal estate and to hold sweet communion with Me, your Father in Heaven, when I will teach you all things you desire to know.

I have been picturing the Impersonal estate from many view-points, in order that it may become so familiar that you can unerringly distinguish it from all inferior states, and may learn to dwell consciously in it at will.

And when you can consciously dwell in it so that My Words when and wherever spoken can always find lodgment and understanding in your mind, then will I permit you to *use* certain faculties I have been awakening in you. These faculties will enable you more and more clearly to see the Reality of things, not only the beautiful and lovely qualities in the personalities of those about you, but their weaknesses, faults and shortcomings, as well.

But the reason you are enabled to see these faults and shortcomings, is not that you may criticize or judge your brother, but that I may arouse in you a definite resolve to overcome and suppress such faults and shortcomings in your own personality. For, mark you!—You would take no note of them in others were they not still in your self; for I, within, then would not need to call them to your attention.

As all things are for *use*, and *use* only, let us study into the use you have hitherto made of other faculties, gifts and powers I have given you.

You must realize by this time *I* have given you *all things*. All you have, or are, be it of good or evil, of blessing or suffering, of success or failure, of riches or lack, *I* have given you or attracted to you.—For why? For USE— in awakening you to a recognition and acknowledgment of *Me* as The Giver.

Yes, all things you possess have their use. And if you are not conscious of such use, it is only because you can not yet acknowledge Me as The Giver.

And you could not honestly acknowledge Me as such until you *knew* I AM, The Giver. Your personality, in fact, had become so engrossed in trying to get rid of or to exchange many of the things I had given you for other things you thought were better, that of course you could not even dream, much less acknowledge, Me, *Your Own Self*, as The Giver.

But possibly you do now acknowledge Me as The Giver, as the Inner Essence and Creator of all things in your world and in your life, even of your present attitude towards these things.

Both are my doing, for they are but the outer phases of the process I AM using in the expression of My Idea of your inner Perfection, which Perfection being My Perfection is gradually unfolding from within you.

As you more and more realize this, will the true meaning and *use* of the things, conditions and experiences I send be revealed unto you. For you will then begin to glimpse My Idea Within, and when you glimpse that Idea will you begin to *know* Me—your own *Real* Self.

But before you can truly know Me, you must learn that *all* things I give you are *Good*—and that they are for *use*, My use,—and that you personally have no interest in or actual right to them, and they are of no real benefit to you, only as you put them to such use.

I may be expressing thru you beautiful symphonies of sound, color or language, that manifest as music, art or poetry, according to mortal terminology, and which so affect others as to cause them to acclaim you as one of the great ones of the day.

I may be speaking thru your mouth or inspiring you to write many beautiful Truths, which may be attracting to you many followers, who hail you as a most wonderful preacher or teacher.

I may even be healing thru you divers diseases, casting out devils, making the blind to see and the lame to walk, and performing other marvelous works which the world calls miracles.

Yes, all these I may be doing thru you, but of absolutely no benefit is any of it to you personally, unless you use and apply these harmonies of sound in your every spoken word, so that to all hearers they will seem as the sweet music of heaven; and unless your sense of color and proportion so manifests in your life that only kind, uplifting, helpful thoughts flow from you, proving that the only true art is that of seeing clearly My Perfection in all My human expressions, and of allowing the quickening power of My Love to pour thru you into their hearts, picturing to *their* inner vision My Image hidden therein.

Likewise no credit attaches to you, no matter what wonderful Truths I speak or works I perform thru you, unless you, yourself, *live* these Truths, daily, hourly; and make these works serve as a constant reminder of Me and My Power, which I ever pour out freely for you, My Beloved, and for all, to use in My Service.

You, to whom I have apparently given none of such gifts and who deem yourself unworthy and not yet advanced enuf to serve Me in such ways,—to you I would say:

Just to the extent that you truly recognize Me within and seek in real earnestness to serve Me, just to that extent will I use you—no matter what your personality, no matter what its faults, tendencies and weaknesses.

Yes, I will cause even you who thus seek to serve Me to do many wondrous things towards the quickening and awakening of your brothers to a like acknowledgment of Me. I will cause even you to influence and affect the lives of many of those whom you contact, inspiring and uplifting them to higher ideals, changing their way of thinking and their attitude towards their fellows and therefore towards Me.

Yes, *all you* who seek to serve Me, no matter what your gifts, will I make to be a vital force for good in the community, altering the mode of life of many, inspiring and molding their ambitions and aspirations, and altogether becoming a leavening influence in the midst of the worldly activities in which I will place you.

But you at the time will probably know nothing of this. You may even be still longing to serve Me, and hungering for a more intimate consciousness of Me, thinking you are doing nothing, are still making many mistakes and failing to live up to your highest ideals of Me; not realizing that this longing and hungering is the avenue thru which I pour forth My Spiritual Force, which being wholly Impersonal, is used by you, unconscious of its being *I within you* using it, to bring about My Purpose in your heart and life and in the hearts and lives of My and Your other Selves.

And so, as you finally grow into the realization of all this, as you surely will, and *prove* it by the practical *use* of all you have in *My* service, will I gradually give you the strength and ability consciously to use *Impersonally My* Power, *My* Wisdom and *My* Love, in the expression of My Divine Idea, which is eternally striving to manifest thru You Its Perfection.

Therefore will you soon see that your human personality, with all its faculties, powers and possessions, which are in reality Mine operating and manifesting thru you, is likewise for My use wholly, and that true success and satisfaction can never be found except in such use.

For such use develops, as the planted seed develops the harvest, the ability consciously to use *all* My spiritual faculties in the final perfect expression of My Idea, which can be expressed only thru your human personality.

XII.

SOUL MATES.

Let us now examine into some of the things I have given you, those especially of which you cannot yet acknowledge Me as the Giver.

Perhaps the particular position in life you now occupy you do not think the best adapted for the expression of My Idea surging within you.

If so, then why not step out of that position into the one of *your* choice?

The mere fact that you cannot or do not do this proves that at this time such position *is* the one best suited to awaken in you certain qualities necessary for My perfect expression, and that I, your own Self, AM compelling you to remain therein, until you can recognize my Purpose and Meaning hidden within the power such position has to disturb your peace of mind and keep you thus dissatisfied.

When you recognize My Meaning and determine to make My Purpose your purpose, then and then only will I give you the strength to step out of that position into a higher I have provided for you.

Perhaps the husband or the wife I have given you, you think is far from being suited to you or one capable of helping along your "spiritual" awakening, being only a hindrance and detriment, instead. And you may even be secretly contemplating leaving or wishing you could leave that one for another who sympathizes and joins with you in your aspirations and seeking, and therefore seems more nearly your ideal.

You may run away from my first choice, if you will, but know that you cannot run away from your own personality; that, in its selfish craving for a "spiritual" mate. can attract only one who will force you to a ten-fold longer and harder search among the illusions of the mind, before you can again awaken to the consciousness of My Voice speaking within.

For a sympathetic and appreciative mate would only feed the personal pride and selfish desire for "spiritual" power in you, and develop further the egotistic side of your nature; while an unsympathetic mate forces you back upon yourself and compels you to turn within, where I abide.

Likewise, a loving, trusting, yielding mate would encourage only selfishness and conceit, when you are not yet abiding in the consciousness of My Impersonal Love; while a tyrannical, suspicious, nagging mate provides the soul discipline you still need and teaches the value of opposition and self-control.

Did you but know it, the one who is assuming the part of your present mate is in reality an Angel from Heaven, even as are You, one of the Attributes of My Divine Self, come to you to teach you by domination and opposition, by extreme selfishness and unkindness,—which are but the *shadows* of qualities *in you* that the Light of My Idea within, shining thru your clouded personality, casts upon the Soul of your mate, darkening, fettering, binding it to *Its* personality, at the same time magnifying and distorting these shadows of qualities in Its personality so that they stand forth boldly, flaunting before you their power to disturb and harass you,—to teach you that only when you have purged your own personality of these qualities so that My Holy Love can express, can you be freed from the conditions which now are causing you so much disturbance of mind and unhappiness of Soul.

For not until this sorrowing, fettered Soul, this Angel from Heaven, this other part of My and Your Self, who has come to you and is beating Its wings against the barred cage of Its personality in which you are helping to keep It locked; while It all the time is yearning and striving to call into expression thru you the Impersonal Love, the tender, thoughtful care for others, the poise of mind and peace of heart, the quiet, firm mastery of self, which and which alone can strike off the fetters and open the doors, so It can step forth into the freedom of Its own glorious Being and be to you Its own *true* Self,—not until you can see this Soul in all Its Divine beauty, but now sickened and weakened by this earthly bondage, will it ever be possible for you to find and recognize that Ideal you seek.

For that Ideal exists not—without, in some other personality,—but only within, in your Divine Counterpart, which is I, your Higher, Immortal Self. And it is only My *Idea* of this, your Perfect Self, striving to express and become manifest thru your personality, that causes you to see the seeming imperfections in the mate I have given you.

The time will come, however, when you cease to look without for love and sympathy, appreciation and spiritual help, and turn wholly to Me within, that these seeming imperfections will disappear; and you will see in this mate only the *reflection* of qualities of unselfish love, gentleness, trust, a constant endeavor to make the other happy, that will then be shining brightly and continuously from out your own heart.

Perhaps you cannot yet wholly believe all this, and you still question that I, your own Self, am responsible for your present position in life, or that I chose for you your present mate?

If so, it is well for you thus to question until all is made plain.

But remember, I will speak much more clearly *direct* from within, if you but turn trustingly to Me for help. For I ever reserve My Holiest secrets for those who turn to Me in deep, abiding Faith that I can and will supply their every need.

To you, however, who cannot yet do this, I say, if your own Self did not place you here or provide this mate, *Why* then are you here? and *Why* have you this mate?

Think!

I, the ALL, the Perfect One, make no mistake.

Yes, but the personality does, you say. And the personality chose this mate, and perhaps has *earned* no better position.

But what, *who*, caused the personality to choose this particular one and earn this particular position in life? And *who* picked out and placed this one where you could thus choose, and who caused you to be born in this country of all countries and in this town of all towns in the world at this particular time? Why not some other town and a hundred years later? Did your personality do all these things?

Answer truly and satisfactorily these questions to yourself, and you will learn that I, God, within you, your own Self, do all things that you do, and I do them well.

I do them while expressing My Idea, Which is ever seeking manifestation in outer form as *Perfection* thru you, My living Attribute, even as it is in the Eternal, within.

As for your true "Soul Mate," which you have been led by others to believe must be waiting for you somewhere, cease looking; for it exists not without in some other body, but within your own Soul.

For that within you which cries out for completion is only your sense of Me within, yearning for recognition and expression; I, your own Divine Counterpart, the Spiritual part of you, your other half, to which and which alone you must be united, before you can finish that you came on Earth to express.

This is indeed a mystery to you who are not yet wedded in consciousness to your Impersonal Self; but doubt not, when you can come to Me in complete surrender, and will care for naught else than union with Me, will I disclose to you the sweets of the Celestial Ecstasy I have long kept in reserve for you.

XIII.

AUTHORITY.

To you who still feel the desire to read books, thinking in them to find an explanation of the mysteries that now hide from you the meaning of the earthly expressions of My Idea, I say:

It is well that you seek thus outwardly, following the impulses I send, for others' interpretations of the meaning My Idea is expressing thru them; for I will make that search to be of benefit to you, tho not in the way you imagine.

It is even well for you to seek in ancient teachings, philosophies and religions, or in those of other races and other peoples, for the Truth I wish to express to you; for even that search will prove not unprofitable.

But the time will come when you will realize that the thoughts of other minds and the teachings of other religions, no matter how true and beautiful, are not what I intend for you; for I have reserved for you thoughts and teachings which are yours and yours only, and which I will give to you in secret—when you are ready to receive them.

And when the time comes, as it inevitably will, when you become dissatisfied in your search among the teachings of the various religions, philosophies and cults that now are interesting you, and you grow discouraged at finding yourself no nearer the attainment of the powers and spiritual growth so authoritatively described and supposedly possessed by the writers of the books, the teachers of the philosophies and the promulgators of the religions,—then will I show you that while all these books, teachings and religions were originally inspired by Me, and have done and are still doing their part in quickening the hearts of many, yet for *you* it is now meet that you cease looking to *any outer* authority, and instead confine your study to My Book of Life, guided and instructed by Me within, by Me alone; and, if you earnestly and truly do this, you will find that I have chosen you to be the High Priest of a religion, the glory and grandeur of which will be to all others that have been pictured to your former understanding, as the light of the Sun is to the twinkle of the far distant star.

You will likewise realize that the ancient religions were given to My peoples of long ages past, and that the religions of other races are for My peoples of those races, and that none of these are for you; even tho I brought them to you and pointed out many wondrous things in them that inspired you to a more determined search for Me within their teachings.

But I say to you, these are things of the past and have naught to do with you. The time has arrived, if you can see it, when you must cast aside all accumulated knowledge, all teachings, all religions, all authority, even My authority as expressed in this and My other *outer* revelations; for I have quickened you to the consciousness of My Presence *within*, to the fact that all authority, teachings and religions, coming from any *outer* source, no matter how lofty or sacred, can no longer have any influence with you, only as they become a means of turning you *within* to Me, for My *final* authority on all questions of whatsoever nature.

Therefore, why seek in the things of the past—in religion, human knowledge, or in others' experiences—for the help and guidance which I alone can give?

Forget all that has gone before. That which is past is dead. Why burden your soul with dead things?

Just to the extent you hold to things that are past, do you still live in the past, and can have naught to do with Me, Who dwell in the ever-present NOW, the Eternal.

Just to the extent you attach yourself to past

acts or experiences, religions or teachings, do they cloud your soul vision, hiding Me from you, and which will ever prevent your finding Me; until you free yourself of their darkening influence and step within, into the Light of My Impersonal Consciousness, which recognizes no limitations and penetrates to the infinite Reality of all things.

Likewise the future concerns *you* not. He who looks to the future for his final perfection is chained to the past and can never get free, until his mind no longer is thus engrossed with the consequences of his acts, and he recognizes Me as his only Guide and throws all responsibility upon Me.

You, who are one with Me, are perfect *now*, and always were perfect, knowing neither youth nor old age, birth nor death.

You, the Perfect, have naught to do with what has been or what is to be. You care not for anything but the eternal *NOW*. That only concerns you which immediately confronts you,—how perfectly to express My Idea here and now in the condition in which I have placed you purposely for such expression.

When that has been done, why not leave it behind, instead of dragging it along with you, burdening your mind and soul with consequences which are but empty shells from which you have extracted the meat?

All this applies to re-incarnation, to which belief many minds are fast chained.

What have You, the Perfect, the Eternal, to do with past or future incarnations? Can the Perfect add to its perfection? Or the Eternal come out of or return to eternity?

I AM, and You Are,—ONE with Me,—and always have been, and always will be. The I AM of You dwells in and reincarnates in ALL bodies, for the one purpose of expressing My Idea.

Humanity is my body. In It I live, move and have My Being, expressing the Glorious Light of My Idea thru My Attributes, whose Celestial Radiance to the human vision is bedimmed and distorted by the myriads of clouded and imperfect facets of the human intellect.

I and You, Who are One with Me, reincarnate in Humanity, as the oak reincarnates in its leaves and acorns, season after season, and again in the thousand oaks born from their thousands of acorns and their oaks, generation after generation.

But you say you remember your past lives.

Do you? Are you *sure?*

Very well, what if you do? Just because I have permitted you a glimpse of the Reality of one of My past expressions, that you might the better comprehend My Meaning which I am *now* expressing to you, is no assurance from *Me* that you *personally* were My avenue of that expression.

For do I not express thru all avenues, and You with Me, and are We not the Life and Intelligence of all expression, no matter what the character, or the age, or race?

But if it pleases you to believe that *you* actually were that expression, it is well, and I shall cause such belief to be of benefit to you; but only to the extent of preparing you for the great Realization that afterward will come.

In the meantime you are chained fast. Your personality, with its selfish desires and selfish seeking, is still bound hand and foot to the past, and looks only to the future for its deliverance, after the final wearing out of all the consequences of its acts; dominating your mind and intellect with this false belief in birth and death, and that such is *your* only way to final emancipation and union with Me; preventing the realization of Our Eternal and Ever-Constant Oneness, and that You can free your Self any moment You will.

For it is only the personality that is born and dies, and which seeks and strives to prolong its stay in the body and in earth life, and then to return to other bodies after I no longer have any use for its body.

And it is only to this personality that you are bound, by the beliefs and opinions it has engrafted on you back thru the ages, during which it has kept your human mind busied with such delusions; and it is only when you can rise up in the realization of your Divine Immortality, Omnipotence and Intelligence, and can cast off *all* personal beliefs and opinions,—that you can free your Self from this perverted relation, and can assume your true position as Master and King, One with Me, seated upon the Throne of SELF, compelling the personality to take its proper and natural place as servant and subject, ready and willing to obey My slightest command, thereby becoming an instrument worthy of My Use.

XIV.

MEDIUMS AND MEDIATORS.

To you who, in your desire to serve Me, have joined yourself with a church, religious organization, occult society, or spiritual order, of whatsoever nature, thinking, by aiding in and supporting its work, it would please Me, and that you might receive special favors from Me in consequence,—harken to these My Words and ponder over them.

First, know that I AM already pleased with you, for you do nothing that I do not cause you to do, and you do it to fulfill My Purpose,—altho it may seem to you at times you are acting contrary to My wish and only to satisfy your own desires.

Know likewise that I provide all minds with all their experiences of life, which I utilize solely to prepare the body, quicken the heart, and develop the consciousness, so that they can comprehend Me, and so that I can express thru them My Idea.

I inspire minds with glimpses of Me and My Idea thru these experiences, and I have spoken thus thru inspiration to many, who have taken My

Words and have written them in books and have taught them to other minds. And these Words I have caused to quicken the hearts and consciousness of those who are ready to receive them, even tho the writers and teachers of themselves had no real comprehension of My Meaning.

Many of those whose minds I thus inspire with glimpses of Me and My Idea I cause to become teachers and leaders, organizing churches and societies and cults, drawing seekers and followers to them, that I, thru the words I thus speak thru them, can quicken the hearts and consciousness of those that are ready to recognize Me.

But I, the Impersonal One within, do all this, and the teachers and leaders personally do nothing, only serving as channels thru which My Idea can express to the consciousness of those I draw to them for that purpose.

For the mind is only a channel and the intellect an instrument, which I use Impersonally whereever and whenever necessary to express My Idea; and not until the *heart* has been quickened and has opened wide to contain Me can man, with his mortal mind and intellect, consciously comprehend My Meaning, when I express thru him My Idea.

You, in your desire to serve Me, may have found in some teacher or leader a personality whom you think, from the many seemingly wondrous words I speak thru him, is now containing Me in his heart.

In your doubts and anxiety to please Me, and in your fear of My displeasure when disobeying My commands, you may even have gone to such teacher or leader, who possibly claimed to be a priest or priestess of the Most High, thinking to get thru such My Message to you, or words of advice or help from some "Master" or "Guide" in the spirit side of life, who you thought was My Emissary.

You may go to such, if you will. Aye, it is I who offer you such alternative, if you will not and cannot be content to trust and wait for Me to answer and help in My own time and way.

Yes, I even send you to such, and let you put all your faith and trust in such priest or priestess, letting them feed you with all the "spiritual" advice and teaching from such "Master" or "Guide" you can hold. Until finally, in sorrow and humiliation from the disillusionment which eventually and inevitably follows, you once more are thrown back upon yourself, upon the Teacher within, upon Me, your own True Self.

Yes, all the deception, all the discipline, all the taking of your ardor and devotion—not to speak of your money and services—to what you believe to be My Work, and selfishly purloining and utilizing them for the upbuilding and strengthening of their own personal power and prestige among their followers; feeding each of you with just enuf subtle flattery and promises of spiritual advancement, together with clever sophistry under the guise of high and beautiful sounding spiritual teaching, to keep you bound to them so you would continue to support and honor and glorify them, ever holding over you the lash of My displeasure if they receive not unquestioning trust and obedience,—yes, all this *I* bring to you, for it is what you desire and seek, and Desire is truly the agent of My Will.

You may be even giving to some other teacher, —either in the seen or the unseen, and no matter how true, well-meaning and spiritually wise,—who you think cannot be classed with the kind just mentioned, your unquestioning love, devotion and obedience, and you may be receiving what you think are teachings and guidance of inestimable value.

And all this is well, so long as you are receiving that which you seek and think you need; for I supply all things to satisfy such desires. But know that all such is vain and unproductive of the real results sought; for all seeking and all desire for spiritual attainment is of the personality and therefore selfish, and leads only to final disappointment, disillusionment and humiliation.

But, if you can see it, it is in the disillusionment and humiliation that the real results are attainable, for those are what I opened up for you and led you towards, when presenting the possibility of getting help from some human teacher; and these, disillusionment and humiliation, are what I purposely brought you to, in order that, having become once more humble and docile as a little child, you would then be ready to listen to and obey My Word spoken within, and, hearing and obeying, you could enter into My Kingdom.

Yes, all outward seeking will end thus, and will but bring you back to Me, weary, naked, starving, willing to listen to My Teaching and to do anything for even a crust of My Bread, which in your stubbornness and conceit you disdained before and deemed not good enuf for your proud Spirit.

But now, if you have had enuf of teachings and teachers, and are sure that *within* you lies the Source of all Wisdom, these words will bring joy unspeakable to your heart. For do they not confirm that which you already have felt within to be true?

For you who cannot yet see this and still need a Mediator, I have provided the story of The Christ crucified for your redemption, picturing how I desire you to live that, thru the crucifixion of your personality, you may rise in consciousness to Oneness with Me.

But to you who are strong enuf to bear it, I say you need no mediator between you and Me, for we are One already. If you can but know it, you can come direct and *at once* to Me in consciousness, I, God within you, and I will receive you and you shall abide with Me for ever and ever; even as does My Son Jesus, the Man of Nazareth, thru Whom I AM even now expressing as I did express nineteen hundred years ago, and as I some day shall express thru you.

To you who wonder how and why I say such beautiful and such spiritual things thru personalities who fail to live up to the teachings they apparently of themselves give out, I say:

I use all avenues Impersonally to express My Meaning.

Some I have prepared to be better mediums of expression than others, but personally knowing nothing of Me.

In some I have quickened the heart so as the better to contain Me, thereby becoming consciously more at one with Me.

Some have become so at one with Me that they no longer are separated in consciousness from Me, and in Whom I live and move and express My Spiritual Nature.

Since the earliest days of expression on earth I have prepared My Priests and My Prophets and My Messiahs to vision forth to the world My Idea —My Word that shall finally become flesh.

But whether I speak thru Priest, Prophet or Messiah, or thru a little child, or thru your worst enemy, all words that appeal vitally to you are the words the I AM of *You* speak thru the organism of such medium to your Soul consciousness.

Should a number be gathered together to hear My Word spoken thru one of My Priests, it is not the Priest of himself but *I, in the heart of each* hearer, Who draw from the Priest the vital words that sink deep into the consciousness of each. The Priest knows not what he says that so affects you, and may not even comprehend My meaning of the words he speaks to you.

But I within him do draw from the combined devotion to and belief in Me, consciously or unconsciously expressed by all those gathered around him, the Spiritual Force which serves as a channel or a connecting line thru or over which I reach the consciousness of those minds I have prepared to comprehend My Meaning. For altho I speak the same words to all, yet these words contain a distinct and separate message for each, and no one knows any but the message I speak to him; for I within you choose from the words the meaning I intend for you, and I within your brother and your sister likewise choose the meaning I intend for each of them.

When two or three are gathered together in My Name, there will I always be; for the Idea which draws them together I within each inspire, for it is My Idea. And from the union of their aspirations towards Me do I create a medium or channel thru which I enable the Soul consciousness to gain such glimpses of Me as each is capable of comprehending.

Every Priest, every Teacher, every Medium, I cause instinctively to know this, for they are My chosen Ministers; and I likewise cause to awaken in them a desire to surround themselves with followers, that I may quicken in the hearts of those who are ready a consciousness of My Presence within. The Priest, the Teacher, or the Medium, themselves, may never have recognized Me within, and may be deeming Me as entitized or personalized in some master or guide or saviour *without* themselves; but nevertheless, there are those whom I lead to these, My Ministers, in whom, thru certain words I cause My Ministers to speak, together with the Spiritual Force furnished by the various aspirants, I am enabled to awaken their Soul consciousness to a real comprehension of Me, the

Impersonal One, seated within—in the very midst of All, in the heart of each.

For the I AM of My Minister, and the I AM of each follower is *One*, one in consciousness, one in understanding, one in love, and one in purpose, which purpose is the fulfillment of My Will.

And this I AM, which is wholly Impersonal, and knows neither time, space nor different identities, merely utilizes the personalities of both Minister and followers, and the crcumstance of personal contact, as a means of giving voice to My Idea, ever struggling within for outer expression.

Those Ministers who take the confidence and trust of My followers, and use it to further their own private purposes, I cause to awaken to a recognition of My Will and My Idea all in proper season. This awakening, however, is not pleasant to their personalities, and almost always causes much suffering and humiliation; but their souls rejoice and sing grateful praises to Me when I bring it to pass.

Therefore, wonder not at the sometimes wonderful words of Truth that come from mouths apparently unfit to speak them and comprehending not their meaning; nor at the fact that simple followers oftentimes awaken faster than and grow beyond their teachers. I Who dwell within both teacher and follower choose different conditions and provide different ways for the expression of My Attributes in each different Soul, fitting each into just the time and place where they can complement and help each other the best; thus uniting all into the most harmonious expression of My Idea possible under the circumstances.

XV.

MASTERS.

To you who are still holding to the idea, taught in various teachings, that I will provide a "Master" or Divine Teacher for each aspirant towards union with Me, hear My Words.

It is true I have permitted you in the past to delve into all kinds of mystical and occult books and teachings, encouraging your secret desire to acquire the powers necessary to attain this union extolled in such teachings, even to the extent of quickening in you some slight consciousness of the possession of such powers.

I have even permitted the belief that by practicing certain exercises, breathing in a certain way, and saying certain mantrams, you might attract to you a "Master" from the unseen, who would become your teacher and help you to prepare for certain initiations that would admit you into an advanced Degree, in some secret Order in the inner planes of existence, where much of My Divine Wisdom would be opened up to you.

I have not only permitted these things, but, if you can see it, it was I who led you to these books, inspired in you such desire, and caused such belief to find lodgment in your mind;—but not for the purpose you imagine.

Yes, I have brought you thru all these teachings, desires and beliefs, trying to point out to your human mind the Forces I use to bring into expression My Divine Idea.

I have portrayed these Forces as heavenly Hierarchies, and that your human intellect might the better comprehend, I pictured them as Angels or Divine Beings, Impersonal agents or executors of My Will, engaged in the process of bringing into expression My Idea that was in the beginning.

But you did not understand.

Your human intellect, enamored of the possibility of meeting and communing with one of these Beings, as claimed in some of the teachings, proceeded at once to personalize Them, and began to long for Thei appearance in your life, imagining that They are interested in your *human* affairs, and that by living in accordance with certain rules set down in certain teachings, you could propitiate Them so They would help you to gain Nirvana or Immortality.

Now I have purposely permitted you to indulge yourself with such delusions, letting you long, and pray, and strive earnestly to obey all the instructions given; even leading you on, sometimes, by giving you glimpses, in self-induced visions and dreams, of ideal beings, which I permitted you to believe were such "Masters."

I may even have caused to open in you certain faculties, which make it possible for you to sense the presence of personalities that have passed into the spirit side of life, and who have been attracted by your desires and seek to fulfill the part of Master and Guide to you.

But now the time has come for you to know that such beings are *not* Masters, also that *Divine* beings are *not* Masters; that I, and I alone, your own Real Self, AM the only Master for you;—

That any being, either in human or spirit form, that presents himself to your consciousness and claims to be a Master, or *whom your mind assumes to be a Master*, is nothing more nor less than a personality, the same as yours, and therefore is *not* Divine, as your human mind understands that term, despite the many wonderful "truths" he may utter, and the "marvelous" things he may do.

Now, this is a mystery, and until you can comprehend it, you are justified in claiming the above as not consistent with certain statements herein, and that it contradicts teachings in My other Revelations.

But fear not; this mystery will be revealed unto you—if you truly wish to know My Meaning.

Until then, why, in your seeking, be satisfied with anything short of the Highest?

Why seek in human or spirit teacher, guide, master or angel, for the necessarily *limited* manifestation of My Perfection, when you can come *direct* to Me, God within you, the Omniscient, Omnipotent, Omnipresent, the Inspiring Idea back of and within *All* manifestations?

As I AM in You, even as I AM in any you seek, and as all the Wisdom, all the Power and all the Love they possess come only from Me, Why not now come to *Me*, and let *Me* prepare you also so I can express My All thru *You?*

Just so long as your human mind seeks or worships the *idea* of a Master in any other being, no matter how lofty or sacred he may seem to you, just so long will you be fed with such ideas; until, verily, I may, perhaps, permit you to meet and commune with such a "Master."

But if that "privilege" *is* vouchsafed you, it will be only in order to hasten your awakening and your consequent disillusionment, when you will learn that "Master" is indeed but a *personality*, even tho far more advanced in awakening than you, but still a personality—and not the Divine One your innermost Soul is yearning for you to know.

For I feed you with every idea that will operate to teach you the reality back of the seeming, and if I lead you on to apparent deception and loss of faith in all human teachings, and in all human and even Divine perfection, it is only to enable you the more clearly to distinguish between the substance and the shadow, and to prepare you for that far higher Ideal I am waiting to picture to you.

You can rise in your human personality only to the ideal your *human* mind is capable of conceiving. Thru Desire I cause My Will to manifest in you, and thru Desire I perform many wondrous works.

But you, who have risen above Desire, you who no longer seek a Master or a Teacher, or even Me, but are abiding alone in the faith of My Eternal Presence and Promise,—for you I have in store a meeting and a communion, which will bring to your Soul such joy and blessings as your human mind is incapable of conceiving.

You are a human personality, yet You are Divine and therefore Perfect.

The first of these truths you believe, the latter you do not believe.

Yet *both* are true.—*That* is the mystery.

You *are* just what you *think* You are.

One or the other, *which* are you?—Or both?

You are *One with Me*. I AM in You, in Your human personality, in Your body, mind and intellect. I AM in every cell of Your body, in every attribute of Your mind, in every faculty of Your intellect. I AM the Soul, the active principle of each.

And you are in Me. You are a Cell of my Body; You are an Attribute of My Mind; You are a Faculty of My Intellect. You are a part of Me, yet You are I, My Self. We are One, and always have been.

Your human personality is to You, what You are to My Divine Impersonality. They are Our creations, expressions of Our Being.

You are one of My mental Attributes, one of My Divine Powers, one of the Radiations of My Will, which I send forth Impersonally to accomplish My Purpose.

Yes, *You* are a Divine Being, an Angel of Light, a living Part of Me, which I have willed forth into earthly manifestation in order to express Impersonally My Idea.

Could an Angel, a wholly Impersonal Being, an Attribute of My Will, be interested in human affairs?

No. It only uses your human nature and your human affairs as mediums or avenues thru which My Will can bring into expression My Idea.

And this idea of a Master I brought to your mind's attention was only to lead you to and prepare you for this Idea of Me, your Impersonal Self, an Angel of Light, the *One True Master*, within.

As your human mind is constituted, it at certain times thinks it needs a Master, one to whom it can turn with its human trials and problems for explanation and advice, thinking life's problems can be settled that way. And if I draw to you one who fails you or deceives you and throws you back finally upon Me, your own Self, discouraged, disillusioned and humiliated, it is only that perhaps then you will be ready to turn to *Me within*, and will listen to *My* voice, which all these years has been speaking to you, but to which your proud and egoistic mind has not deigned to listen.

You who have not yet had this experience, who have not yet met the Master of your aspirations, either in human or spirit form; you, within whom My Words have failed to awaken a quickening response to their truth,—for you I have in store certain experiences which will surely lead you to Me later on, and then you will be brought to know that I AM the Master, the *inspiring Idea* back of and within every thought of and every aspiration towards a Master that enters your mind, whether coming from within or without.

If you doubt this, you need only to apply the Key;

To think of a Master *is to create* one.

This idea of a Master, by your thinking, becomes what you desire and imagine a Master to be.

In other words, by your thinking you build around this idea all the qualities you imagine a Master possesses. Your human mind, thru Desire, thru aspiration, thru worship, must needs create these qualities in some *imaginary* being, who is still a personality, for you cannot as yet conceive of an *Impersonal* being.

Therefore, according to the intensity of your desire and thinking, must this idea sooner or later come into actual manifestation, either by attracting to you such a personality in the flesh, or one entitized in the realm of visions and dreams.

It is taught, "When the pupil is ready the Master appears." And this is true, in a sense; but not as you have interpreted it.

Your secret desire for a Master will bring him to you, but only when I have prepared you for such appearance. But such appearance will be only an *appearance* of a Master. The *true* Master or Teacher, when he appears, you may never recognize; for he may be hidden in an interesting friend, a business associate, your next door neighbor, or in your own wife or husband or child.

For I teach thru every avenue needed at the time to impress your human consciousness. And as I am continually teaching you, even when you do not know it. I have many ways of reaching your consciousness, and utilize all to bring you to a realization of My Meaning.

I speak with many voices, with the voice of Fear, Love, Envy, Kindness, Ambition, Drunkenness, Pleasure, Jealousy, Sensuality, Suffering, Shame,—with the voice of all human emotions, passions and desires. I speak with Nature's voice, with the voice of Experience, even with the voice of *human* knowledge.

Yes, these are all My Voice, which I use Impersonally to express to you the *one fact*, that I AM in All and that I AM All; and what this Voice says, in Its thousand ways, is that you, too, are part of this All, and that I AM in *you*, waiting for your recognition of Me and your *conscious* co-operation in the expression of My Idea of Impersonal Perfection on earth, even as It is expressing in Heaven.

When this recognition comes, and then only, will you meet and know the true Master. Then and then only will you realize that I, your own Impersonal Self, AM the only possible Master of your human personality.

Then you will understand why no being, human or otherwise, could be Impersonal and be a Master to any other being; why an Impersonal Being could never be known as a Master to a human being, and therefore could not have any interest in human affairs.

If a being should come into your life, who *seemed* to you Divine, and yet showed an interest in you, be sure he is not yet wholly Impersonal. Such an one might be a Master-Man, but he would not be Divine.

But perhaps you would be satisfied to have such an one for a Master, even if he were not wholly Impersonal. If so, then I would hereafter bring you to a realization of *his* personal imperfections by a constant comparison with *My* Impersonal Perfection; until you would finally turn and come to Me in complete abandon, acknowledging Me and My Impersonality as the only Model and Ideal, and as the true Cause which inspired your long search without for My Perfection, that could be found only within, hidden deep within your own Soul.

XVI.

THE CHRIST AND LOVE.

To you who fear that My Words may destroy your belief in and love for the Lord Jesus Christ, I say:

Nearly two thousand years ago, when the process of the expression of My Idea had reached the stage where I could show forth some of My Divine *Reality*, in order to do this and so as to recall to My human Attributes their mission on earth, it became necessary to express thru a human personality and to manifest in a human form My *Divine* Attributes, so their human minds and intellects could see and remember and be inspired by Me within to let My Idea similarly express thru and manifest in their human personalities.

This I did thru the personality of Jesus, the man of Galilee, picturing to the human understanding by My Teachings given thru Him, and by My *Life* manifested by Him, what was necessary in order to express fully My Divine Idea.

I showed, by the experiences of a symbolic nature thru which I caused his human personality I created for such purpose to pass, what all personalities must pass thru before you, My human Attributes, who created these personalities, can again become Impersonal enuf to be conscious expressors with Me of My Divine Idea.

All of you, My human Attributes, before the I AM within can awaken your human minds to a realization of Me, your Divine Self, must be born of a Virgin Love in an humble manger—the place where the cattle come to feed (in humble faith and trust in God, to which the human or animal nature must come). You must then be taken into Egypt, the land of darkness (or intellectual activity), there to grow and thrive in body and understanding until you become strong with the feeling of Me within. Then, when sufficiently conscious of *My* power and *My* Love, will I begin to speak thru you words of Wisdom and Truth, which will confound the learned of the world, even the Doctors of the Law. Then will follow a long period of study and meditation, which ripens the mind and develops the Soul, until you arrive at full maturity of the I AM consciousness within, and which prepares you for your baptism in the Jordan, when you will be opened completely to Me, to the full consciousness that You and I are One, that there is no separation, that I AM your Real Self; and I AM henceforth permitted wholly to direct your lives.

I then *lead* you out into the world, called in My other Revelation the Wilderness, there to try you and make you strong and to accustom you to the Impersonal use of My Divine Attributes. I bring to you the three great Temptations of Power, Self-Righteousness, and Money, until you have proven that nothing of the intellect, nothing of the self, nothing from without, can tempt you to forget Me within, and that My Voice and Mine alone, whether speaking in your heart or in the hearts of your brothers, is the only Voice you are now capable of hearing.

This proven, there will begin the period of performing miracles and of teaching the multitude, accompanied by the revilement and persecution of the unbelieving and scoffing world; followed by the trial before Pontius Pilate, the representative of the Worldly Law; the sentence; the ascent of Calvary carrying the Cross; the being nailed upon the Cross; the Agony; the three days in the tomb; and then the final resurrection, when you enter into complete union with Me.

All of which has its inner meaning, or Soul application, and which should be readily understood by you, if you have opened your heart to Me.

Such has been The Way in the past for you and for all who have studied and followed My

Teachings, given forth in My former Revelations. But now the time has come when I have prepared you and many for a new Dispensation, wherein you can enter into the consciousness of Me direct and *at once* by the Impersonal Way. Those who are big enuf and strong enuf to throw off all claims of the human personality, and who can say I AM, and *know I AM The ONE within* Who give them this strength and enable them to rise above the attractions and influences of the outer world,— those are the ones I have chosen thru whom to express all the wondrous glories of My Divine Idea.

The Christ, or the I AM Consciousness, must be born in your heart and in the heart of every human personality, must grow and thrive and pass thru in some manner every experience symbolized in the life of Jesus, before you can come to this point and become a conscious expressor with Me of My Divine Idea; and the example of the Christ Love and Compassion which I expressed in that Life must you also express in some degree in your life, before you can taste of the fruits of that Love, which in reality is not love, but the Holy Three-in-One,—Love-Wisdom-Power, that is the true expression of My *Impersonal* Life.

You heretofore have not known the meaning of the Impersonal Life, hence you could not know the meaning of Impersonal Love. Love to you, if you will carefully analyze that feeling, has always been a human emotion or expression; and you have been unable to conceive of a love devoid of or unattached to some human or personal interest. But now, as you begin to feel *Me* within your heart and open it wide to contain Me, will I fill you with a wondrous strange new feeling, which will quicken every fibre of your being with the creative instinct, and be to you a veritable Elixir of Life. For in the outer expression of *that* feeling, when I thus, thru you, pour it forth into the world, will you taste of the unutterable sweetness of My Holy *Impersonal* Love, with its accompanying illumination of mind and consciousness of unlimited Power; and it will make you a wholly selfless and therefore perfect channel for the Impersonal expression of My Divine Idea.

And you will realize that you are part of Me and part of every other being, and that all you have or are, are not yours, but Mine, for Use wherever and however I direct.

And your life will no longer be centered in your self, but that self will be lost, merged in your other Selves, giving freely of your Life, your Understanding, your Strength, your Substance, which are but phases of My Impersonal Life or My Impersonal Love, that I have portioned out to you only for such use.

In the personality of Jesus, the Christ, I manifested much of the Love Impersonal, enuf to inspire and lead you into seeking to emulate His Life and His Personality, and, thru such seeking and striving, to awaken in you the consciousness of the Christ within *you*. Thru this awakening and the realization that the Christ is but the channel or door that opens unto Me, I have finally brought you to the point where you can enter in and consciously become a part of My Impersonal Life.

But I here tell you plainly that My Impersonal Love has naught to do with personal lives and personal loves. All such are but the outer mediums I use thru which to pour from out the heart of Humanity into the world My Real Love, where it is ever expressing its all-embracing, vitalizing, creative, and up-lifting Power.

My Love considers not individuals or personalities; they are but pawns on the chess-board of life which I move as I deem best to accomplish My purpose,—the full and complete expression in Humanity of My Divine Idea.

In Humanity only can I express My Idea, even as you can express your idea of yourself only in and thru your human personality.

In Humanity I live and move and have My Being. It is the mortal personality and body of My Immortal Self, even as is your personality and its body what you use to express your being.

All individual human personalities with their bodies are but the cells of My Body of Humanity. Just as the I AM of you is now building your body so that thru it You can perfectly express My Idea of you, or your Real Self, so am I gradually building Humanity so that thru It I can perfectly express My Idea of My Self.

As the individual cells of My Body of Humanity, even as those of your human body, by partaking of My Life, become Impersonal and harmonious parts of the organs they form, they live a healthy and happy life. But let one cell oppose or act contrary to the general law of its organ, and the harmonious functioning of that organ becomes impossible, which naturally affects the whole body and results in dis-ease.

Every cell of an organ is an integral part of that organ, and its work is necessary to that organ's perfect functioning and to the perfect health of My Body. So that unless each cell gives up *all* its power and *all* its intelligence, which are but attributes of the Life I give it, toward the perfect functioning of My entire Body, the only result for My Body can be inharmony, with its consequent effects,—disease, suffering, sin, bondage, poverty, lack of understanding, disintegration, or death.

Likewise, unless each organ gives up all the intelligence and all the powers with which I endowed it, to the one purpose of expressing and maintaining the life of My Body in perfect health, the only result can be disorganization, disruption, rebellion, and finally WAR,—war between the various organs and between their respective cells, and a greater or less consequent chaotic condition in My whole Body.

In My Body of Humanity this would mean war between Nations, which are the Organs of My Body. And as all war is but acute disease or disharmony, and as My Life, which in Humanity manifests as Impersonal Love, can express only in harmony—even as in the physical body, It is always utilizing, equalizing and preparing conditions so that It can thus express.

This It does either by eradicating gradually from the various organs of the body all diseased, weakened and unfit cells, or by developing the disease into a malignant form—such as fever, dropsy, carbuncles, blood-poisoning, or degeneracy, in the physical body—it throws off such cells quickly by the billions, until a particular organ either is purified or its power of functioning is wholly destroyed.

In other words, the real life and work of each cell and of each organ lies in giving up its individual life that My whole Body can Be or Express in perfect harmony. When each cell and each organ has no other idea than this, and makes itself a pure and selfless channel thru which My Impersonal Life can flow, then has My Body become a harmonious and perfect Whole; and then can My Idea express on earth Its Divine powers and possibilities, even as it does in the Celestial Realm of the Eternal.

As you give up your self wholly to Me that I can pour thru you My Holy, Impersonal Love, having no other thought than the perfect expression of that Love, which is My Real Life, then will I thru you be enabled to quicken and awaken those about you gradually to a recognition of Me, The Christ within *them*, so that they too will likewise give up their selves wholly to Me. Until finally the organ, or that particular part of My Body of Humanity you and they form, attains perfect health and harmony, and adds its quota to the bringing about and maintaining of perfect health in My entire Body.

When such time comes, My Divine Life Force, or My Impersonal Love, will be flowing and manifesting thruout all Humanity, and My Idea will be expressing fully on earth even as It is in Heaven; and the earth and all earthly bodies will no longer be of the gross physical material they formerly were, but they will have become utterly purified and cleansed of the self, and will have been again lifted up to from whence they descended. For the purpose of their creation, that of developing organisms for the outward manifestation and human expression of My Divine Idea, will have been accomplished; and having no further use for physical or outward mediums of such expression, I hereafter will create and express only with Mind Substance, which is the only medium needed in the Heavenly World of the Impersonal Life.

XVII.

FINDING ME.

To you who have studied carefully all that has been said herein, and who think you have gotten a glimpse of Me, but yet are not sure, come close, and listen with your Soul to what I now have to say.

Be still!—and KNOW,—*I AM*,—GOD.

If you have learned to "Be Still," if you have studied and meditated upon this "I" as God within you, if you are able to distinguish it from the personal I, and are conscious at times of being able to step outside, as it were, of your personality and view your human self as it is, see all its petty faults and weaknesses, its base selfishness, its animal appetites and passions, its childish desires and foolish pride and vanities;

If you can do all this and have seen these things with clear vision, know that at those moments you have been One with Me in consciousness, that it was your Real Self, I within you, permitting you thus to see with My eyes the Reality of things.

At those moments you were freed from your personality and were dwelling in My Consciousness, call it Cosmic, Universal, Spiritual or Impersonal Consciousness, as you will; for you could not have seen these things in your self excepting thru Impersonal eyes, My eyes.

Again, if you will look back you will recall many times when you felt strongly impelled to do certain things, some of which you did, with perfect results; others of which you argued against, your intellect reasoning you into different action, and always with failure, disappointment or suffering as a result.

This impelling consciousness was only your Real Self, I within you, at such moments guiding you, distinctly telling you what to do. At those moments you were hearing with your Spiritual ears, My ears, and when you Impersonally obeyed, success and satisfaction followed, but when you personally thought you knew better, discomfiture, regret and unhappiness resulted.

Again, there have been moments when you have *felt* approaching events, or the nearness of unseen persons, or inharmonious vibrations when contacting others.

This is only the Real you feeling with your Spiritual or Impersonal Body, whose consciousness, did you but know it, is ever on the alert to protect and warn and advise you regarding all outer things, conditions and events.

But the best and surest way you may know Me is when Selfless Love fills your heart, and there is a strong, compelling urge to help some one, to heal their ills, to relieve their suffering, to bring them happiness, to point out the True Way,—that is the actual feel of Me within you, pushing the personality aside, using your mind and body for the purpose I created them, as avenues for the expression of My Real Nature, which is Perfect Love, the Christ of God, the one, vitalizing, quickening, life-giving, strengthening, healing, all-supplying, all-informing Power in the Universe.

All this is pointed out to you in order to impress upon you that it is I, in your Spiritual body, the Perfect body within, where I dwell, Who am always thus talking to you, advising you, teaching you, warning and helping you, in all the affairs of life, yes, in every little detail.

And if you will but turn to Me, and will carefully watch for and study these impressions which you are receiving every moment, and will learn to trust them, and thus to wait upon and rest in *Me*, putting all your faith in Me, verily I will guide you in all your ways, I will solve for you all your problems, make easy all your work, and you will be led among green pastures, beside the still waters of life.

Ah, My child, if you will spend but one-tenth of the time and energy you have wasted in seeking without among the husks of human knowledge and human teachings, in earnest, determined efforts directed within to find Me;

If you will devote but one hour each day thus to Me alone, imagining and practicing the Presence of Me within you;

I here promise you that you will not only soon, very soon find Me, but I will be to you an exhaustless fount of such Wisdom and Strength and Help, as your human mind now cannot possibly conceive.

Yes, if you will but seek Me thus, making Me FIRST in your life, never resting until you do find Me, it will not be long before you will become conscious of My Presence, of My Loving Voice, speaking constantly from out the depths of your heart.

And you will learn to come to Me in Sweet Communion, and gradually you will find yourself abiding in My consciousness, and that My Word is abiding in you, and that whatever you desire will in seemingly miraculous ways be done unto you.

But this abiding *continually* in Me will be difficult at first, for the World, the Flesh and the Devil are still in evidence in your consciousness. But you will gradually become accustomed to the use of My Impersonal Eyes, and will soon be able to see into the Reality of things, even into the Reality of these seeming Lords of the Earth; when you will find you are dwelling in a wondrous *new* World, peopled with Angelic Beings, using the Flesh bodies of their human personalities merely as vehicles, or instruments, or clothing, in which to contact the earthly conditions and experiences they have created, in order to develop the Soul qualities necessary for the perfect expression on earth of *My Idea.*

To your eyes then there will be no shadows, no evil, and consequently no Devil; for all is Light and Love, Freedom, Happiness and Peace, and you will see *Me in all*, in each Being some attribute of Me, in each animate thing some phase of Me; and you will need only to let My Love shine from out your heart and it will illumine for you the Real meaning of *all* that you see.

And then the great Realization will come, that you have found the Kingdom of God, that you are walking in it, that it is right here on this earth, that it is manifesting all around you, that you have been living in it all the time, but you did not know it;

That instead of being without in some far off place, it is within your own being, within every other being, the innermost inner of all manifested things.

In other words, it will be found to be the REALITY of ALL things, and that all outward seeming is but the shadow of this Reality, created by man's misconceptions and his belief in his separateness from Me.

And when you have found The Kingdom, you will likewise find your place in It, realizing now that you are in truth one of My Divine Attributes, that your work was all laid out for you from the beginning, and that all that has gone before has been but a preparation and a fitting of your human personality for that work.

And your whole Soul will leap with joyful anticipation, that, after all these many years of wandering, you have at last returned to My Home, and can now enter into My Real Life, One in consciousness with Me and with your other Selves, all working to bring about the final perfect expression on earth of My Divine Idea.

To you who the reading of this has brought memories of previous joys and whose Soul has quickened in response, do not leave these words until you have gotten from them all I have to tell you. Be Still! and listen to My inner Voice, and learn of the glories that await—if you are able to see with Impersonal Eyes and hear with Impersonal Understanding.

But if this reading brings to you your first vision of My Reality within you, setting in motion, by this partial realization of Me and My Kingdom, high vibrations which lift you into a temporary Spiritual ecstasy, and you resolve to try to abide always in this consciousness of Me, and always to obey Me, —do not be discouraged should you fail ignominiously when immediately thereafter an occasion comes to test the sincerity and strength of your resolve.

For it is only by your trying and failing and realizing keenly your lack of strength and ability to rest and trust in Me, that I can quicken in you the consciousness of My Divine Powers ever waiting to manifest thru you.

These high vibrations are only the arousing into action of certain *Soul* qualities and their corresponding faculties, which must be awakened before I can manifest such Powers.

And naturally when such Soul qualities are aroused, they call into active opposition certain other qualities which heretofore held undisputed sway in your nature, and which must be overcome and brought under subjection and then lifted up into their true service before the Soul qualities can freely express.

And this opposition is merely in order to strengthen and test and perfect the expression of these Soul qualities, for they must be capable of withstanding every attack from without before they can fully manifest all My Divine Powers pushing forth from within.

But know I am manifesting these Powers in you just as fast as you can bear it and be strong.

The mistake you make is in trying to grow yourself.

I AM the Tree of Life within you. My Life will and must push forth, but it will do it by gradual and steady growth. You cannot come into your fruitage before you have grown to it. But remember, My Life is all the time building you up into the perfection of health and strength and beauty, that must express outwardly as it is even now expressing within.

You who have begun to realize I AM within, but have not yet learned to commune with Me, listen and learn now.

You have learned to "Be Still," and you have perhaps *felt* My Presence within. If so, realizing *I AM* there, ask Me a question. Then, with a silent, earnest prayer to Me for an answer, but without anxiety, care or personal interest, and with mind a perfect void, wait confidently for the impressions that will come.

Should a thought come in answer that you recognize as what you have heard or read somewhere, cast it out immediately, and say, "No." Father, what do *You* say?

Other thoughts may come from other human sources, but if you are alert you will recognize them as such and refuse to accept them. And then, if you *persist* in asking *Me*, you will finally get an answer that you will *feel* is really from Me.

Thus it will be *at first*. When you have learned to distinguish *My* Voice from all other voices, and can keep your personal interest wholly suppressed, then will you be able to hold silent communion with Me at will, without interference from others' ideas, beliefs and opinions; and you can ask any question you wish, or another can ask you any question on any problem on which they need help, and *I will that moment place in your mind the words to speak*, either silently to yourself, or audibly thru your tongue to the other.

You, My Beloved, who have consecrated your self to Me, and are bending every effort to find union with Me, but instead have found apparently that every prop of the World's support has been withdrawn or is being withdrawn, and that you are without money and without friends and know not where to turn for human help;

Learn, My Blessed One, that you are very, very

close now, and that if you will only continue to abide in Me, letting My Word abide in and guide you, resting and trusting absolutely in My Promise, I will very soon bring to you a Joy, a Fulfillment, a Peace, that human words and human minds can not possibly picture.

For you have obeyed My Commands, and you have *trusted* Me, and have sought first My Kingdom and My Righteousness, and therefore will I add all other things unto you, even those the World has denied you.

But you, my Dear One, who likewise have consecrated your self to Me, but who are still holding to some of the World's standards, being unable to let go and trust wholly to Me;

You to whom, therefore, I have brought failure, disappointment, even poverty, in order to teach you the real value of all worldly things, their impermanence, their lack of power to provide happiness, their having nothing to do with My Real Life;

You, dear child, who cannot yet see this and your heart is full of anxiety and fear because you cannot see where tomorrow's bread is coming from, or the money for next week's rent, or for the past due mortgage;

Listen once more to My Words long since given to you in the Sermon on the Mount.

"Therefore I say unto you, Take no thought for your life, what ye shall eat or what ye shall drink; nor yet for your body, what ye shall put on.

"Is not the life more than meat, and the body than raiment?

"Behold the fowls of the air; for they sow not, neither do they reap, nor gather into barns; yet your heavenly Father feedeth them. Are ye not much better than they?

"Which of you by taking thought can add one cubit unto his stature?

"And why take ye thought for raiment? Consider the lilies of the field, how they grow; they toil not neither do they spin; and yet I say unto you that even Solomon in all his glory was not arrayed like one of these.

"Wherefore, if God so clothe the grass of the field, which today is and tomorrow is cast into the oven, shall he not much more clothe you, O ye of little faith?

"Therefore take no thought, saying, What shall we eat? or What shall we drink? or Wherewithal shall we be clothed?

"(For after all these things do the Gentiles seek) For your heavenly Father knoweth that ye have need of these things.

"But seek ye first the kingdom of God, and His righteousness; and all these things shall be added unto you.

"Take, therefore, no thought for the morrow, for the morrow shall take thought for the things of itself.

"Sufficient unto the day is the evil thereof."

Do you need any more definite Commands or any more definite Promise than these?—You who have consecrated yourself to Me, and call yourself My disciple.

Listen!

Have I not always provided everything? Have you ever been in need but what I always appeared with help just at the right moment? Has there ever been a time when things looked dark that I did not bring Light?

Can you, with what you know now, look back over your life and see where you could have ordered it better? Would you exchange your *Spiritual* understanding for the earthly possessions of any one you know? Have I not done all this, despite the fact you have been rebelling and refusing to listen to Me all your life?

Ah, My Children, can you not see that money, home, clothes, food, and their acquirement, are only incidents, and have nothing to do with your *real* Life, excepting as you make them real by thinking into them so much importance, and letting Me remain only a side issue?

And if it becomes necessary for Me to take the things of the world away that you may learn the Truth,—that I AM the *only* important thing in Life, that I *must* be *FIRST* if you *truly* love Me, —I do this—as does the true physician who, in order that the patient may be assisted to health, first removes the *cause* of disease—that *real* and *lasting* Happiness and Prosperity can be yours.

And this applies to you also, My Child, you who have lost health, have lost courage, have lost all hold of your Self, and after weary years of seeking without from earthly physicians and remedies, following faithfully every instruction and suggestion given, in order to regain the Life you have lost,—you who have turned finally within to Me, with the faint hope that I may be able to help you.

Know, My Little One, that you, too, must come in complete surrender to Me, the One and Only Physician who can heal you. For I AM the Life Omnipotent within you. *I AM* your Health, your Strength, your Vitality. Not until you can *feel* *ME* within, and know I AM all this to you,—real and lasting Health is not for you.

And now, My Children, draw close. For I AM now going to tell you the means of obtaining all these things—Health, Prosperity, Happiness, Union, Peace.

In the following words lie hidden the Great Secret. Blessed be you who find it.

Be still! And KNOW,—*I AM*,—GOD.

KNOW I AM *in you.* KNOW I AM *You.* KNOW I AM your *LIFE.* KNOW *All* Wisdom, *All* Love, *All* Power abides in this Life, which is flowing freely thru your entire being *NOW.*

I AM the LIFE, *I AM* the INTELLIGENCE, *I AM* the POWER in *all* Substance, —in all the cells of your body; in the cells of all mineral, vegetable and animal matter; in fire, water and air; in Sun, Moon and Stars. I AM that in you and in them which IS. Their consciousness is One with your consciousness, and All is My consciousness. Thru My consciousness in them All that they have or are is yours—for the asking.

Speak to them then IN MY NAME.

Speak in the consciousness of your Oneness with Me.

Speak in the consciousness of My Power in you and of My Intelligence in them.

Speak—COMMAND what You WILL in this consciousness,—and the Universe will rush to obey.

RISE UP! O ye aspirant for union with Me. Accept now your Divine Heritage! Open wide your Soul, your mind, your body, and breathe in My Breath of Life!

KNOW that I AM filling you full to overflowing with My Divine POWER, that every fibre, every nerve, every cell, every atom of your being is *now consciously ALIVE* with ME, alive with *My* Health, with *My* Strength, with *My* Intelligence, with *MY* BE—ING!

For I AM *within* you. We are not separated. We could not possibly be separated. For I AM *You*. I AM your *REAL* Self, your *REAL Life*, and I AM manifesting My SELF and *ALL MY POWERS* in you *NOW*.

AWAKE! Rise up and assert your Sovereignty! *KNOW* your SELF and your POWERS! KNOW that *all I have* is yours, that My Omnipotent LIFE is flowing thru you, that you can take of IT and build with IT what you WILL, that IT will manifest for you as Health, Power, Prosperity, Union, Happiness, Peace,—anything you *Command!*

Imagine this. THINK it. *KNOW* it! Then, with all the *Positiveness* of your nature, *Speak* the *Creative WORD!* And it will not return to you void.

But know, Beloved, that this cannot be until you have come to Me in complete and utter surrender, until you have given your self, your substance, your affairs, your Life into My keeping, putting all care and responsibility upon Me, resting and trusting in Me absolutely.

When you have done this, then will the above Words quicken into active life My Divine Powers latent in your Soul, and you will be conscious of a Mighty FORCE within you, which, just to the extent that you abide in Me, and let My words abide in you, will free you entirely from your Dream World, will quicken you fully in Spirit, will make all the way clear for you, supply all things you desire, and lift trouble and suffering from you for evermore. Then will there be no more doubts and questionings, for you will KNOW that I, God, your very Self, will always provide, will always point out the way; for You will have found that *You and I are One.*

XVIII.

UNION.

To you who truly wish to consecrate yourself thus to Me, and are willing to give your *whole* Life to Me, putting aside all personal ideas, hopes and aims, in order that I may freely and fully express thru you My Impersonal Idea, listen carefully to these Words.

I have led you thru all your experiences of life up to just this point. If you are now really ready and willing to serve Me, and have learned that you, of yourself, can know nothing and can do nothing, and that I AM, and what you call *your* intelligence and *your* strength and *your* substance is really Mine, and that it is I who direct all your thoughts and both cause and enable you to do all that you do,—then can you comprehend the significance of My Words, and are quite prepared to obey them.

I have hitherto brought to you the experiences that would teach you just these things. But now, if you are ready and worthy, you shall work *consciously* with Me, joyfully yet calmly awaiting each new experience, knowing that in each is contained marvelous expressions of My Meaning, which I will make altogether clear to you, and which will more and more bring you into loving, intimate union with Me.

Thus all experiences will hereafter be blessings, instead of trials and tests, or karmic effects of previous acts; for in each will I disclose unto you glorious visions of My Reality—of your own True, Wonderful Self; until you no longer will have any disposition to follow any of the old desires, but will seek only to know *My* wishes and to please *Me*.

This will manifest in many new ways. In your activities, be they what they may, you will care not what the task, doing whatever lies before you, knowing that is what I require; and striving always and only to please Me by your *Impersonal* part in the doing, which enables Me thus to accomplish *speedily* My Will.

In your business even, you will find I AM there. In fact, it is I Who provide you with such business, *whatever* it be; not that in it you can be the success or the failure or the common plodder you are, nor that you can pile up riches for your descendants, or lose all that you have, or never accumulate any. No, but that thru the success or failure, or lack of ambition or special ability, I may quicken your heart to a realization of Me, the Impersonal One, seated within; inspiring and directing all these things that you do, waiting for you consciously to participate in the *true* Success and accept of the *real* Riches I have in store for you.

You will then learn that your business, or labor, or condition of life, are but incidents, or the outer vehicles I choose and use to carry you thru the certain experiences which I deem best adapted to bring you to this realization; and at the same time to quicken in you certain Soul qualities that now but imperfectly express.

If you can but *know* Me, dwelling thus in your heart, accompanying you to your office, to your shop, to your labor, whatever it be, and will permit Me to direct your business and all your ways; verily I say unto you, when you can do this, you will at once become conscious of a new Power within you, a Power that will flow forth from you as a gentle, kindly sympathy, a true brotherliness, a loving helpfulness to all with whom you come in contact, inspiring them to higher principles of business and of life, creating in them a longing to shed a similar influence within their own circle; a Power that will attract to you business, money, friends, an abundance of all things you *need;* a Power that will connect you with the highest realms of thought, enabling you both to vision clearly and to manifest consciously all My Impersonal Powers and Attributes every moment of your life.

And you will no longer feel any need to go to

church or to religious meetings of any kind, or even to read the teachings of My Revelations, in order to find Me and to worship Me.

Instead you will turn *within* and always find Me *there*, and you will be so filled with the joy of communing with and serving Me, and of *thus* worshipping Me, that you will care not for any other thing than just to listen to and obey My Voice, and to feel the warmth and thrill of My Tender Love, as it fills and surrounds you and prepares the way and softens the conditions wherever you go and whatever be your work.

You I will cause to be an uplifting and leavening influence in the community wherever I send you, drawing all men to Me to receive My Blessing thru you, who now are able so to subserve your personality to My Holy Impersonality that they forget you and see only Me, and feel the quickening of My Presence within their own hearts; so that they go forth with a new light in their eyes and the sense of a new purpose in their lives.

In your homes particularly will I dwell. Thru those nearest you will I teach you many wonderful things, which now you can understand, when before you passionately rebelled against their truth. Thru husband, wife, child, brother, sister, parent; especially thru the tyrant, the scold, the selfish, will I now be able to develop in you these great qualities,—patience, gentleness, forbearance, tongue-control, loving-kindness, true unselfishness, and an understanding heart; for I will cause you to see that I, deep down in *their* hearts, am compelling their personalities to give just what your personality calls forth thru the weaknesses in it that still exist.

Now will you be able to appreciate this and profit by it. And when you truly do comprehend this great truth will you be able to see *Me* in your brother or your wife or your parent or child, appealing to you with loving, sorrowing eyes, when they speak thoughtlessly or selfishly or in the heat of anger. Instead of blaming them you will turn *within* to Me, the Impersonal One, Who will speak thru you gentle words of loving kindness, which will immediately soften the heart of the other, and bring you once more together, and closer than ever before. For I, the *real I*, in the heart of each, am One, *and always respond when thus called upon.*

Yes, if you can but know it, your greatest school and your greatest teacher is in your own home, by your own fireside. Much, very much is reserved for those who consciously know this and permit Me, the Impersonal One within, to do the teaching. For I will not only teach you many things thru the mouths of those nearest you, but I will teach those others similarly thru you. But with this difference,—if *you are conscious* of Me and

Impersonally are resting in Me and My Wisdom, then *you* will permit *Me* to choose your words and to direct your acts, and you will care neither for their effects upon others or upon yourself, putting all responsibility upon Me.

When you can do this, you will marvel at the changes you see taking place, both in your personality and in the personalities of your dear ones—until you are able to see, back of their human personalities, Me, your own Impersonal Self, shining from out their eyes.

When you *can* thus see Me, then will the heavens be opened unto you, and no more will you see flaws in your brother, or hear inharmony around you, or feel unkindness coming from any other fellow being. For you will *know* that I, the Impersonal One, within that other, AM the fount of all perfection, of all harmony, of all loving-kindness, and wait but for the human personality to make the recognition, step submissively aside, and let My Light shine forth, resplendent in all the glory of My Divine Idea.

Then will you see that all conditions in which I put you are the places I have chosen where you can best serve Me; that in all places and in all conditions there is much, very much to do, the more objectionable they are to the personality the more need there be of My Living Presence.

Wherever you are when the awakening comes, whatever has been your training,—in business, in a profession, in manual labor, in the church, or in the underworld,—there lies perhaps your best opportunity to serve; for there you know best the manner and the way. For how can My and Your other selves awaken to a knowledge of My Presence within, without the quickening influence which must first come from without. You who have received must give. You who have been quickened must become the quickener. You must take into this business, into this profession, into this labor, into this underworld, My Living Presence, must open the doors of the saddened and sickened hearts and let My Light and My Healing Love pour in. You must supply the leaven that will leaven the lump. It these conditions are to be lifted up, you, My awakened one, must carry to these, My ignorant and betrayed ones, My inspiration, My blessing, My strength, that they can rise up and throw off the influence of the world's ways, can harken to My Voice within, and can hereafter be the master of surrounding conditions and no longer the slave. No condition in life can be lifted up or conquered by running away from it. The Divine touch is needed and must be supplied. But it can only be supplied by one who has sounded the depths as well as reached the heights of human experience, with *Me* as Guide and Interpreter.

You who read, and whose Soul comprehends, are blessed, and your work lies before you.

But you who still hesitate while your personality quakes in fear as the Light filters thru your clouded intellect,—you, too, will soon partake of My Blessings; for I am rapidly preparing you for the joy that awaits.

But both you who comprehend and you who fear, know that I AM even now manifesting My Will thru you; and the time will surely come when you will know no other Will but Mine, and when all things *You* Will, will come to pass.

But this will not be until you, yourself, have become one with Me; until there is nothing left in *your* human personality to attract from others the slightest inharmonious thought or feeling, by act or word of yours. Your way *then* will be one continuous round of blessing. Wherever you go will My Light shine and My Love radiate forth about you, creating Peace, Concord, Unity. And the great thing will be, tho not great but natural when once you understand, that every one will be better and happier by reason of your appearance in their lives. For the I AM in them, while still in the flesh, has found or sensed within *you* a truly Impersonal avenue of expression, and therefore feels, tho not consciously by the personality, the Glory and the Holiness of My Impersonal Life.